A DEATH BY ARSON

Following an eventful Christmas, Euphemia Martins, like her employer Richenda Muller, is looking forward to a quiet start to 1913. But their hopes are dashed when Richenda's husband Hans announces that they are to visit the home of Sir Richard Stapleford, Richenda's nefarious twin. Sir Richard is holding a grand party at his Scottish estate to celebrate the New Year, and Hans is looking to seal a business deal or two. The Muller household, plus Richenda's brother Bertram, soon discover that Richard has rather a big surprise up his sleeve . . . But murder follows Euphemia like night follows day; and when a body is found, she investigates — only to find herself under suspicion. Meanwhile, Richenda is decidedly (and calamitously) off cake — and Bertram is overjoyed at the technological progress of the motor car . . .

SPECIAL MESSAGE TO READERS

Libraries and Information

This book should be returned by the last date stamped above. You may renew the loan personally, by post or telephone for a further period if the book is not required by another reader.

119886 Designed and Produced by Wakefield Council. Communications 09/14 ↻recycle

www.wakefield.gov.uk

wakefieldcouncil
working for you

7 0 0 0 0 0 0 0 3 3 9 2 1 0

A DEATH BY ARSON

A EUPHEMIA MARTINS MYSTERY

CAROLINE DUNFORD

ISIS
LARGE
PRINT

First published in Great Britain 2016
by
Accent Press Ltd

First Isis Edition
published 2019
by arrangement with
Accent Press Ltd

A catalogue record for this book is available
from the British Library.

ISBN 978–1–78541–715–3 (hb)
ISBN 978–1–78541–721–4 (pb)

Published by
F. A. Thorpe (Publishing)
Anstey, Leicestershire

Set by Words & Graphics Ltd.
Anstey, Leicestershire
Printed and bound in Great Britain by
T. J. International Ltd., Padstow, Cornwall

This book is printed on acid-free paper

Opening Note

This story takes place directly after the
Christmas short story *What the Dickens?*

CHAPTER ONE

Hans' holiday plans

It had all begun peacefully enough. We had been a small and happy family party at the Mullers' estate. Christmas of 1912, with its attendant shocks, was past. Richenda's adopted daughter, three-year-old Amy, would never be left alone ever again — especially if there was an open window nearby and a snowy roof to explore. My very dear friend Merry, Amy's nursemaid at the time, had been unceremoniously dismissed by Hans, and was thus hovering on destitution[1] when her long-term beau, the chauffeur Merrit, asked her to marry him. His employer, my old friend Bertram Stapleford, had given him a cottage on the estate with this very idea in mind. That she would now be called "Merry Merrit" had not dimmed her happiness one wit. I knew that once she was ensconced on Bertram's damp estate in the heart of the Fens it might be some time before I saw her again, but considering how the story could have ended it was an excellent outcome, though I would miss her sorely.

In general, servants do not have the luxury of indulging in travel. My lot has been different, but then as the

---

[1] A feeling I was once all too familiar with.

granddaughter of an Earl, albeit incognito — and with the advantage of a decent education by a learned and beloved father and the disadvantage of having no money and a mother and little brother to support — I have always been out of the norm. I have even — though strictly I am not allowed to speak of it — worked for King and Country. I have scaled the heady heights of service, going from maid, with upstairs responsibilities, to housekeeper, and have finally settled as companion to Richenda on the Mullers' lovely, modern estate.

Richenda once locked me in a cupboard, but I try to remember that at the time she was under the influence of her vile twin, Sir Richard, whom I (together with Bertram, their half-brother) was attempting to prove guilty of patricide. Although Richard was arrested, no charges were brought and he is now, perhaps fittingly, an MP. In Parliament he shouts, blusters, does countless deals, and has grown fat. I wish him all the worst.

Which is why Hans' announcement was so very shocking,

"You want me to go to Scotland in January?" screeched Richenda. "Scotland? To spend time with *Richard*?"

"I believe," replied her husband, "that the country prides itself on its New Year celebrations."

"They call it Hogmanay," I added unhelpfully.

It was the day after Boxing Day. The snow, so thick in the week before Christmas, had vanished from the estate leaving a damp chill in its wake. We had, in the end enjoyed a small family celebration, with Bertram staying for the festivities. Amy's delight at her presents had brought the cheer that only a small child can to

Christmas. It was thus a total and very unwelcome surprise to Richenda and me when Hans announced we were shortly to embark on a journey to Richard Stapleford's new estate, Peterfield, and that Peterfield was in Scotland.

"I have already accepted on our behalf," said Hans calmly. "Your brother has made it clear, my dear, that he wishes to be reconciled with you. He is holding a New Year's party, so we will hardly be alone with him. I gather it is to be quite the glittering affair."

"Did you know about this?" Richenda turned on Bertram. Caught in mid-sip of his coffee, Bertram choked in a way that gave him away completely.

"You did!" I cried. "I suppose you even agreed to Christmas here so you could travel up with us!"

This was both an unfair and geographically foolish accusation, as Bertram's estate was far further north than the Mullers', but a tell-tale blush crept over his face. "Oh my goodness," I said, "you wanted to arrive in a party — not on your own." Bertram gave me a furious look before turning his attention to his shoes, so he did not have to meet his half-sister's gaze.

"Strength in numbers," said Hans, ever the diplomat. "I feel much the same myself."

"Why on earth did you accept?" asked Richenda.

"I have already told you, my dear."

"I don't believe that for a minute," said Richenda bluntly.

"There will be many people at the party," said Hans, obviously unwilling to say more.

"Is this to do with business?" Richenda's voice rose once more to a screech. "*Business?* How could you be so vulgar, Hans!"

"I say, see here," muttered Bertram in protest. Richenda quelled him with a look.

"The truth, Richenda," said Hans, and, for once, his voice took on a steely note, "is that we owe our living to my business interests and that your father made his fortune in business."

"I hold shares in the Stapleford bank," said Richenda, turning her argument around in a moment, "Are those and the estate not enough to sustain us?"

"I am not a man to live off his wife," said Hans coldly, his eyes sending Richenda the clear message that this was something better discussed in private.

Richenda, as ever, missed the point.

"Admirable though that may be, husband," she said, "I do not like my brother. I do not wish to go to Scotland."

"I have accepted," said Hans, with what I, at least, could hear was a finality which would not be brooked.

"This is not a good time for me to be travelling!" cried Richenda, and then to everyone's surprise and embarrassment she burst into tears and fled from the room.

Hans looked as uncomfortable as I have ever seen him. He is usually the most unperturbable sort.[1]

"Well, yes," said Bertram, indulging in the annoying habit of coughing that he does when he is unsettled,

---

[1] He needs to be, married to Richenda.

"you could hardly expect her to love the plan, old chap. Perhaps you should have given her a little more warning."

"And spoil Christmas?" said Hans sharply. Then he sighed and turned to me. "I am sorry to have sprung this on you, Euphemia. I know your history with Richard Stapleford is not a happy one.[1] But I am afraid I am indeed using his connections to meet some business people at the party, people who I have not been successful in engaging with recently."

Bertram and I exchanged looks. Hans is a merchant banker. He is also half-German — and it was a time when Germany was viewed with increasing hostility. I should add that there is nothing vaguely Germanic about Hans, except for his blond hair. In all else he is the perfect English gentleman.[2]

Bertram, irritatingly, coughed again. "There's no need to explain to us, old chap."

"Why are you going?" I asked him, both to divert attention away from Hans' embarrassment and because I was genuinely curious. "You don't owe Richard a thing. Nor are you involved in banking."

"I asked him," interjected Hans. "I thought it would make all our lives easier."

---

[1] Only a diplomatic sort like Hans could have understated this so vastly.

[2] This may be the problem. Hans combines diplomacy and charm, where other English gentlemen usually combine boorish behaviour and schoolboy banter.

I regarded Bertram thoughtfully. "That was very kind," I said. Bertram coughed again. "Though I do wish you would stop doing that," I snapped.

Bertram looked at me as might a puppy that had been unexpectedly kicked. I suppose another woman might have found him sweetly attractive at that moment. At least he had finally shaved off his dreadful beard, and it had taken a decade off him.

"I think I might take some air," he said with as much dignity as he could muster. Outside I could hear the sort of drizzling rain that makes leaves drip endlessly and soaks through any coat in minutes. I gave him an incredulous look. Bertram nodded to Hans and left.

"You are a little unkind," said Hans gently. "He is doing me a great favour."

"You mean that people who might not easily talk to you will do so in his company?"

Hans looked pained. "I do not believe that needed saying, Euphemia."

"I am sorry, Hans," I said. "You are right. I was rude. I am upset you did not confide in me earlier. I could have helped Richenda accept your plan and avoided this scene."

Hans' handsome face broke into a smile. He reached out and touched my hand lightly. "My dear girl, there is nothing anyone — even you with your mighty powers of persuasion — could have done to make Richenda happy about this."

He did perhaps leave his hand on mine a touch longer than was necessary. Hans and I have an affection for one another that is perhaps not common between employer and employee, but there has never been the slightest suggestion of impropriety on either side. But it was unfortunate that at that moment, Rory McLeod — Bertram's butler, and the man who had jilted me — walked into the room.

He took in the situation at one glance and his face became a mask of fury.

"What the hell is going on?" he demanded.

CHAPTER
TWO

Not everything can be blamed on cake

Hans stood and faced Rory. He is one of the few men who can match Rory for height. "I have no idea how your relationship with Mr Stapleford works, but in my house no one, least of all someone else's servant, addresses either Miss St John or myself in that manner."

Rory hesitated. "I take it you are still in Mr Stapleford's employ?" asked Hans, his voice as cutting as I have ever heard it.

"Aye," said Rory, "and it was only a few days ago yous were saying if I ever needed a situation you'd hold one open for me for life." It was a good rejoinder, but knowing Rory as I did, I could see he realised he had overstepped the mark.

"Perhaps then I did not know what manner of a man you were," responded Hans.

"If you will excuse me, Hans, McLeod," I said, rising and making my exit from the room. However, the two of them resolved the situation I knew my presence could not help.

It was with a feeling of shameful relief that I climbed the stairs to the first landing. I was considering where I might go and how long I should give for the occupants of the house to cool their spirits when I almost fell over Richenda.

She was lying diagonally across the landing. Her eyes were closed and she was not moving. It says a lot for my career history that the first thing I did, without even thinking about it, was check she was still breathing. It was only when I was assured of this that I screamed.

I have a loud and carrying scream. In mere moments Rory and Hans were panting by my side. The garden door opened and I heard Bertram's voice call, asking if it was the lunch gong already. Neither Rory nor Hans bothered to reply to him. Between them they lifted Richenda — the observation that neither of them could have lifted her unaided was silently acknowledged.

"Take her to her room," I said to the men, who were already doing so, "I'll send for a doctor."

Bertram pounded up the stairs. "Good God! Is the old girl all right? She's not . . .?"

I tapped him on the shoulder and made him descend the stairs before me. I seriously doubted he would be of any help. "No," I said softly to him. "She appears to have fainted."

"Richenda doesn't faint," said Bertram bluntly. "It's not the kind of thing she believes in."

As Richenda was an out-of-doors, horsey kind of woman, who was overly fond of cake, and usually blunt to the point of self-endangerment, I would have agreed with him — if it hadn't been for the very obvious fact that she just had.

"Well, she has now," I said. "I am going to telephone for the doctor."

"Do you know how to?" asked Bertram doubtfully.

"It cannot be that hard," I said. I had never before had occasion to use the telephonic apparatus. "I can always ask Stone to do it for me."

"I'll do it," said Bertram with the heartfelt relief of a man who has found a way to be useful in a difficult situation. "You should be with her. Get her maid and get the cook to make up whatever it is women have when they faint. What is that?"

"I have no idea," I said. "Though perhaps her maid will have some smelling salts to hand."

"Burnt feathers," said Bertram. "That's what my mother used to use. I'll get some feathers from the garden after I've called the doctor."

At least, I thought, it would give him something else to do. I hurried upstairs, hoping fervently that Richenda's sudden indisposition would have diverted Hans and Rory from their disagreement.

When I reached her room, I found they had laid her on the daybed. Hans was kneeling by her side, patting uselessly at her hand and calling her name. He looked up at me. "I have rung for her maid," he said in a despairing voice. Rory hung back by the door. I sent him away to the cook to "fetch what was necessary". I had no idea what might help Richenda, but Rory, who can be the perfect butler when he wishes, would no doubt have more idea than I. He gave me a startled look in response to my curt command and left sharply. Richenda's maid entered with a small glass bottle. I took it from her, and gently easing Hans aside I uncorked it under Richenda's nose. At once a vile ammonia smell arose. I slammed the stopper back in at once before my breakfast had occasion to revisit me. Richenda stirred, coughed and said, "Jupiter, why must you always wait until we are back in the stable? You bad boy!" Then she opened her eyes. I stepped back. Hans, in a most undignified way, threw his arms around his wife. Richenda squeaked in surprise. I turned my back so I would not see this unusual display of affection.

"Good heavens, Hans! What on earth has come over you?" asked Richenda, sounding entirely like her normal self.

"Oh my darling girl," said Hans in tones that made me blush. "You gave us such a fright."

I heard the sound of Richenda scrambling to sit up and decided it was time I rejoined the conversation. I turned round to see her, pale, but sitting steadily upright. "Euphemia?" she asked.

"I found you on the landing," I said. "You had fainted."

"Nonsense," said Richenda. "I don't believe in fainting."

"Well, it appears, my dear," said Hans in his more usual accent, "that fainting believes in you."

Richenda frowned and I thought I saw a flash of concern in her eyes. "Hans, my dear, would you mind leaving me for a little while? I think I need some rest."

Hans rose at once. "Of course, my darling. But promise me you will ring the bell if you feel unwell in the slightest."

"I shall keep Euphemia with me," said Richenda. She nodded to her maid. "You may go."

When we were alone, Richenda said, "You need to get me a doctor."

"One is on his way," I said. "Hans insisted one was called the moment you were taken ill."

A smile flickered over her lips and for once Richenda looked almost pretty. She would never be beautiful, but when she was happy there was a glow about her that was appealing. "He was the gallant, wasn't he?" she said. "I can almost forgive him for dragging us to Scotland."

"Oh, I don't think he will continue to insist upon our going, now," I responded. "He is far too concerned for your well-being."

"Oh Lord, no," said Richenda. "Now we will absolutely have to go. Damn it!"

Before I could ask her what she meant by this extraordinary about-face, Bertram erupted through the door, brandishing a handful of pigeon feathers. "Will these do? Am I too late?" he gasped. His colour was high and a sheen of sweat covered his face.

"Sit down," commanded Richenda, sounding quite like her normal self. "Euphemia, loosen his cravat! Heavens, Bertram, what do you mean running around like that? You will bring another of your dizzy spells upon yourself." The words were sharp, but Richenda's tone was surprisingly gentle.

"Thought you needed these," said Bertram, sinking down onto one of the overstuffed chairs Richenda favoured in her boudoir.

"Feathers?"

"Mama used to have them burnt when she fainted."

"Your mother never fainted in her life," said Richenda. "She was a formidable actress."

Rather than taking offence, Bertram smiled at her. "Well, you seem to have gone one better for once, Rich."

Rory entered with a glass of brandy on a tray. "Give it to him," said Richenda, nodding at Bertram. "He needs it more than me."

Rory placed the tray on a table and took over from my unsuccessful attempts to loosen Bertram's cravat. There was an expression of concern on his face. I was close enough to hear him say, "Again, sir?"

"No," said Bertram softly. "Just a little dizzy. All the fuss."

Rory stood and addressed Richenda. "Might I suggest, ma'am, that Mr Stapleford is also seen by the doctor."

"Of course," she said, looking Bertram over. "Might be an idea to go and hurry him up a bit. You can drive, can't you, McLeod?"

Rory nodded briskly and left the room. I passed the brandy to Bertram, though by now I rather fancied it myself.

"What is up with you?" Bertram demanded of his sister.

"I could ask you the same thing!"

"I asked first," said Bertram.

Richenda's face reddened. "I think perhaps," I interrupted quickly, "it might be best if we wait for the doctor to determine your respective ailments. I am sure in the first instance he would advise rest."

"If I go to my room," said Bertram, as ever accurately following my line of thinking, "McLeod will fuss over me like a damned mother hen."

Richenda gave a little chuckle. "That I would like to see," she said.

"Well, Bertram, you can hardly stay here while the doctor examines Richenda," I said. "You could wait in the smoking room, if you think you could manage the stairs."

"I'm not a ruddy invalid," said Bertram, rising. "Send him to me when she's done with him." He stalked out of the room.

"He is, you know," said Richenda when he was gone. "A ruddy invalid. That heart condition of his seems to be getting worse and worse."

"It's strange," I said, "there have been times in the last few months when I have seen Bertram endure extreme circumstances and nothing untoward has occurred."

"Perhaps the thought of losing another member of the family in such a short space of time was a bit too affecting. Though personally I'm quite grateful for the thinning of the pack. If only Richard had the condition instead of Bertram."

My father would have been shocked, but there was a part of me that could not help echoing her sentiments, so I kept my peace. I sat down on a chair. "Perhaps it's because he's getting fatter," said Richenda abruptly. "He was never much of a horseman and I can't imagine that horse-riding is the sport of choice around his estate, among all those marshes."

"I had noticed his collar looked a little tighter," I said. "Perhaps he could take up bicycling?"

Richenda and I looked at one another as the image of Bertram on a bicycle flashed through our minds. Then we both burst out laughing. Richenda laughed so much she began to hiccup. Tears rolled down my face.

The door opened and a man I had never seen before entered carrying a black doctor's bag. He must have been in his early thirties and he was astonishingly handsome. He had the fine chiselled features of a silent movie star and wide, soft brown eyes. "Mrs Muller?" he said, addressing Richenda, "I am Dr Glover. I have recently taken over the local practice. I believe you are recovering from a fainting fit, which your husband assures me is quite out of character." His voice was a pleasant baritone and as soothing as any patient could hope for.

Richenda blushed scarlet. "Indeed, Doctor. I believe I know the cause . . ." She glanced over at me. "Euphemia, if you would please leave me with the doctor."

Dr Glover raised an eyebrow in surprise and even I felt a little twinge of attraction. "It would be normal to have another lady present," he said.

"That won't be necessary," said Richenda firmly.

"Perhaps you might wait outside, Miss . . .?"

"St John," I supplied.

"Well, perhaps you might wait outside, Miss St John; in case Mrs Muller decides she does require your presence."

"Of course, Doctor," I said. I was not entirely sure of the proprieties of the situation. If Dr Glover had been, as he should have been, a man in his mid-fifties with a walrus moustache, I would have had no qualms about leaving her. But I thought Dr Glover was quite a different matter, and I suspected Hans might feel the same.

I had expected to find Hans pacing up and down the corridor outside, but I had reckoned without the English gentleman's fear of ladies' indispositions. There was no sign of him. Presumably, he was relying on me to send for him the moment he was required.

While I did not exactly press my ear to the door — even I would not stoop that low, unless King and Country required — I confess I did strain my ears, but all I heard was the low murmur of voices and at one point the outrageous sound of a giggle from Richenda. Regardless of my orders I was about to step inside the room, when Dr Glover opened the door.

"Come in," he said. "Mrs Muller has something to tell you."

Richenda was sitting propped up on the daybed, a cushion under her ankles and a huge smile plastered across her face. She waited until Dr Glover had closed the door and then she announced, "Congratulate me, Euphemia. I am pregnant!"

CHAPTER
THREE

Uninvited interruptions

I opened my mouth to answer this unexpected declaration when there was a long, loud ring at the front door downstairs. Whoever was ringing the bell was not a model of patience, because I had barely regrouped my thoughts before the bell rang again. This time the sound lasted even longer.

"I had better find Stone," I said.[1]

Richenda sat up in alarm. Her face paled immediately. She whispered urgently, "You mustn't tell anybody!" and sank back down onto her cushions with, I felt, a touch too much melodrama.

"Of course not," I said. "You will want to break the news to Hans yourself." Richenda appeared to be on the point of saying more, but the doorbell rang again and I hurried off to find Stone.

He was standing in the doorway of the smoking room looking as torn and indecisive as it is possible for

---

[1] While there was no etiquette problem with my seeking out the butler — provided he was above stairs — there was no way I could open the front door myself: something I had never managed to explain properly to Richenda.

a man of his stoic disposition to appear. "The door, Stone!" I said.

Stone looked behind him. I peered past and saw Bertram reclining on a sofa, his cravat still loosened and his feet on a stool. Stone appeared to be in the midst of some internal struggle. Finally he said, "Have you seen Mr McLeod, ma'am?"

"No, but he would hardly take it upon himself to open the door of Mr Muller's house."

Stone's eyes swivelled until they were almost at the back of his head. I sighed. "I will stand guard," I said. "Now please get the door before the caller wears out both the bell and my patience."

I never speak harshly to Stone. He is an exemplary servant, so the words were barely out of my mouth before I regretted them. However, Stone's highly polished, squeakless shoes had already glided off down the hall to attend to his duty.

Bertram looked around and saw me. "Got rid of my watchdog, have you?" he said with a smile. "I'm not sure if he was protecting me from further ailment or if he feared McLeod would return to finish what he started."

"Rory started?" I asked confused. I came over and moved his footstool to a slightly more comfortable position.

"It seems we have become notorious in this household for our tiffs. Stone assumed my indisposition was McLeod's fault."

"And you did not correct him."

"Well, he did not actually say as much," admitted Bertram, "and to be honest I did not want Hans and McLeod bringing whatever argument is currently between them in here. I have a devil of a headache."

"What did the doctor say?"

"The usual. Rest. No alarms or excitement. No red meat."

"That bit is new."

"Yes — new man, new-fangled ideas."

"Well, if it helps," I said.

"Good God, Euphemia, you can't expect a man to live without his steak!" He leaned forward. "Tell me, what's up with Richenda? It's not her heart too, is it? She has been putting on weight recently. I haven't dared to say anything, but it cannot be good for her health. I heard her positively panting as she climbed the stairs yesterday. You need to speak to her about it. Either that or ban your cook from making cakes."

"Should I do so, I believe it would be my life that would be foreshortened," I said seriously.

Bertram laughed. "I take it if you can joke, then Richenda is in no serious danger."

"No, she is not, but I believe she will tell you the whole story herself."

Bertram looked most alarmed. "I say, there is no need to go that far! A woman's body and all that . . ."

Considering the group who now appeared at the doorway to the smoking room, this was a most unfortunate ejaculation of Bertram's. Stone had returned, bringing with him a woman I judged to be in her mid-thirties and a slightly older man. The two bore a strong resemblance to each other, but while the woman wore a discreet and tidy dark dress, the man wore a loudly checked suit, a flat cap and an eye-wateringly coloured waistcoat.

"I don't rightly know if I can leave you here, Susie, if this is the kind of treatment you will be exposed to," said the man in an aggressive tone.

"Mrs Ellis and her brother, Mr Brown," intoned Stone. "Mrs Ellis is to be the new nursery maid."

This speech confused me. Was it now the custom for one to refer to a nursery maid as Mrs, as it was with a housekeeper? Or was Hans also to employ her husband? In which case, who was Mr Brown?

"Hang on there," interrupted the man. "I'm not liking what I'm hearing. Who are you?" he demanded of me.

"I am Bertram Stapleford," said Bertram rising to his feet. "Brother-in-law to the owner of the estate, Mr Hans Muller."

"Yeah, but who is *she*?" demanded Mr Brown, gesturing at me.

Bertram flushed slightly. "Take them to Mr Muller's study, Stone," he said.

"I tried to, sir, but it seems Mr Muller is occupied with Mrs Muller."

"So that's what you call it around here, is it?" said Mr Brown rudely. "Come on, me girl. We're out of here."

"I shall be delighted to show you the door," said Stone in a voice admirably devoid of sarcasm.

"Oh, Henry, hush," said Mrs Ellis. She came forward into the room towards me. "I do beg my brother's pardon. I had an unfortunate experience at my last situation and he is being over-protective. I am Susie Ellis, a widow, and I am most eager to secure this appointment."

Bertram offered Susie his hand. "A pleasure," he said. "But neither myself nor Miss St John here can confirm your appointment. You had really better wait in Mr Muller's study."

"I don't know that I like the idea of my sister waiting on a man in his room," said the objectionable Mr Brown.

"I can assure you that Mr Muller is the model of propriety," I said acerbically. "This is a well-run and moral household. It is also unnecessary to ring the doorbell for such an extended period of time."

"I told you we should have used the trade door," said Susie, colouring in embarrassment. "I am so sorry for disturbing you, ma'am."

"I assume your brother is not also looking for work?" I asked.

"Oh no, ma'am. He's in trade. Runs his own grocery shop, he does."

"In that case might I suggest, Stone, that you take Mr Brown below stairs, where he will doubtless be more comfortable, and offer him some ale. I will escort his sister to see Mr Muller and remain with her during the interview. I assume this will relieve your worries, Mr Brown? Afterwards, I will bring your sister to you to say farewell, if Mr Muller sees fit to offer her the position. I assume you have an appointment?"

"Well . . . no," said Susie. "I saw the advertisement in *The Lady*, just before Christmas. I did write, but when I received no reply, what with us being so near and Henry having his van, I thought we could come down and enquire."

"Indeed," said Bertram, his eyebrows rising almost into his hairline. "In that case I am unsure whether Mr Muller will see you at all. Perhaps you might enquire, Stone?"

"I will go up and see them," I interrupted. "Mrs Muller has been taken ill and her husband is attending her."

"Is it typhoid?" demanded Mr Brown.

"It is a mild indisposition," I said coldly.

I left Stone and Bertram to deal with this extremely odd couple. It was true that we were in dire need of a nursery maid now that Hans had forbidden Merry to go near Amy, and with Richenda pregnant and subject to fainting fits we would be much overstretched. Still, my instinct told me that the best course of action would be for Hans to turn these two away. Susie Ellis might have reasonable manners, but her brother was deplorable.

I met Hans on the landing, emerging from Richenda's room. He did not have the happy smile I would have imagined an expectant father to have; instead he frowned at me, "She will not tell me what is wrong. She says you know and will reassure me it is not serious."

"It is not," I said, confused. "But I am at a loss as to why she has not told you the whole story."

"As am I," said Hans stiffly. "It seems there is an issue of trust."

"I am sure it is not that," I said quickly. "I will speak to her. First, I am afraid, we have a situation. A Mrs Ellis has turned up to apply for the position of nursery maid. Leaving aside the fact she has made no appointment, she seems unobjectionable — although they came to the front door."

"They? She has a husband with her? I have no mind to house —" began Hans.

"No, she is a widow and escorted by her brother, a coarse and rude man. He says she has had some trouble in her last position — and I must confess the snippet of conversation they overheard between Bertram and myself would not have been inspiring."

Hans gave a small smile. "I can imagine."

"Please don't," I said. "I promised to escort Mrs Ellis to your study and stay with her during any interview, should you agree to see her."

"And her loutish brother?"

"Taken below stairs by Stone and given some ale."

"Hmph," said Hans. "We are in need of a maid for Amy, but this does not sound promising."

"Indeed," I said. "I did not take to them."

"Well, I suppose I should see what she is like before I send her on her way," said Hans. "To be without a situation at this time of year must be hard, and if she left her last situation under a cloud, then . . ." He stalked off down the stairs with me following, and again marvelling over how very kind Hans can be. I only hoped that his empathy for his inferiors would not lead him into making a serious mistake.

CHAPTER
FOUR

Bertram's foreboding

"So you see, sir, I am well qualified."

We were in Hans' study. Susie had refused a seat and I could tell sitting while a woman was standing made Hans feel very comfortable. He glanced at the sheet she had handed him.

"These are all your references?"

"Not my last position, as I explained to Miss St John. I had to leave in a hurry." She lowered her voice. "I'm afraid the elder son of the house had taken quite a shine to me, and I was not brought up to behave in such a manner."

"How old was he?" asked Hans.

"Seventeen," said Susie.

"A difficult age, to be sure. But he was surely not in your charge?"

"He had two little sisters, aged three and four. Most of my experience, as you will see, is with small children. I'm afraid I was not able to do more than list addresses for most of my references, but you will see my last-but-one position has a telephone number against it and the master and mistress there said they would speak for me."

"You left there why?"

"Their little boy — I'd been with him since he was a baby — turned seven and was sent away to school."

"And Mr Ellis?"

"Mr Ellis died some time ago," said Susie, looking down. "We had only been wed a month. An accident when we were sightseeing in Bath. We were on a late honeymoon. We hadn't been able to go at once as Alf couldn't get time off from his work. It was my fault; I wanted to go there. Neither of us was used to streets that busy — and it all happened so quickly." She brushed a tear from her cheek. "I was hardly Mrs Ellis at all, really, but I kept the name. It was the only bit of him left to me."

Hans coughed uncomfortably and I knew he was thinking about the loss of his own first love. Susie thought differently. "I assure you, sir, I am no wailing widow. I have accustomed myself to my lot in life, and my greatest aspiration is to find another secure post where I may help look after a child or even children. I find their company inspiring."

I met Hans' gaze and, with difficulty, suppressed a smile. Engaging although young Amelia was, *inspiring* was never an adjective I would have used to describe her. Hans raised an eyebrow, clearly thinking the same thing.

"And your current situation?" he asked.

"I am living with my brother." The tone in which the poor woman said this gave a clear indication that she did not consider this ideal. "He has several small children," she added.

26

Comprehension dawned on Hans' face. "Might we ascribe your brother's assertiveness to a reluctance to lose you from his household? Unless, of course, he is seeking work as well. In which case he will be sadly disappointed."

Susie shook her head vigorously. "Oh no, sir. He's not looking for work. He and his wife run a greengrocery business. He is well set up."

Well enough, no doubt, to afford his own servants, I thought to myself. I was beginning to have a great deal of sympathy for Susie, and yet, there was something that bothered me about her. But each time I tried to pin it down it eluded me further.

"Shall we say a month's trial? Subject to my telephoning your reference? Although we are shortly to depart for Scotland. You have no objection to travel, I hope?"

"I have never been abroad," said Susie, her eyes very wide.

"The Scots may be a very different people to the English, but it is hardly abroad."

"In that case, sir, I would very much like to accept your offer of a trial."

"I shall telephone now and see if I can speak to your reference. Euphemia will take you to the morning room and arrange for a tea tray."

"My brother . . ." began Susie.

"Stays below stairs," finished Hans.

I could not be sure but I thought I detected an expression of relief on Susie's face. In what seemed like no time at all the matter was settled. Her trunk had been retrieved from the van by the ill-tempered brother and carried upstairs. I watched her go with some misgiving. "Did you not think Richenda might like to interview her?" I asked Hans, trading on our long-standing acquaintance.

"I just telephoned her former employers. Her reference was excellent. And, frankly, it does not matter what Richenda or I feel. It will be down to how she relates to Amy. I am satisfied she has the ability to keep the child safe. Now all we need to know is if she can keep her under reasonable control."

"Reasonable?" I queried.

"I am not a man to ask for miracles," said Hans gravely, though his eyes twinkled.

"About Merry —" I began.

"No!" Hans held up his hand. "I will not discuss this with you. She is to return to Bertram's estate with Merrit when we depart."

"Will Bertram not require his car?"

"Ah — I have arranged a little late Christmas present for my brother-in-law."

I quailed inwardly. Bertram behind the wheel of his current contraption was terrifying enough, but with one of the new automobiles, which were rumoured, incredibly, to be able to do far more than twenty miles per hour, I felt no road in England would be safe. I could only hope that Rory was accompanying us north, and that he would be at the wheel, but I decided not to push my fortune and ask Hans if that would be so. The last I had seen, the two men had been at extreme odds.

"Perhaps you should tell Richenda the good news?" I suggested. "It might cheer her spirits." It occurred to me that Hans might cancel the whole trip when he learned of Richenda's delicate condition, and that if that was to be so then the sooner the better. I recalled from my days as a housekeeper the enormity of moving a household to Scotland — and that had been only to a small hunting lodge, not a grand New Year's party. I thought it very likely we would not be going, which did not disappoint me in the least. Although I will own that the scenery up there is breath-taking, all my forays northward have occasioned sudden demises. Scotland, Richard Stapleford and a big party of important people might seem like a cocktail of delight for many young women — for I knew that Hans would insist I attend the ball — but I could only think of it as having potential for yet more morbid disaster.

"I think it is better she gets her rest before the journey," said Hans. "I have spoken to the doctor and he says there is no cause for alarm."

I studied him hard when he said this, but he gave no indication of being a man who knows his wife is in the process of producing his heir. Hans continued, "I know you are thinking I should curtail the trip, and that business is not a good enough reason to —"

"I would not dare suggest such a thing," I interrupted.

"No," said Hans, smiling, "but you might well think it. The truth is, Euphemia, that while this trip is important to me — very important on the business front — it would be impossible for us to stay in the house for the next week."

"Why so?"

"I have arranged for the installation of electrical lighting throughout the entire building. I understand that in doing so the men will make a devil of a mess, not to say noise, and that the place will be quite uninhabitable. Now, if you will excuse me, I have matters to attend to."

I watched him go, wondering what on earth I should do. I decided to beard Bertram in the smoking room and get his thoughts on current matters. Whether I should tell him about Richenda's delicate condition, I was unsure. I felt very strongly that it was Hans' right to know first — well, first after Richenda! But it was certainly not my place to tell him; perhaps talking with Bertram, even if I did not expose the secret, would help me decide what to do.

I had barely stepped inside the door when Bertram leapt to his feet. "Oh no," he said. "You are not supposed to be in here."

"Don't be silly," I said. "I was in here earlier with Mrs Ellis and her awful brother."

"That was different," said Bertram. "Totally different."

"What on earth is the matter? You are becoming quite heated."

"It's that look on your face," said Bertram, pointing at me as one might point at the spectre at the feast. "It means we're in for trouble."

CHAPTER
FIVE

Bertram is overcome

The first thing I thought when I saw the car was how very much better Hans must be doing in business than he had led us to believe. Bertram wandered around it in awe. Every few moments the phrase "I say . . ." burst from his lips, but he hadn't yet managed to lengthen it to a full sentence. He circled the vehicle several times before gingerly approaching it like a man creeping up on a sleeping lion. He touched the front of the automobile and looked astonished when it didn't disappear under his fingers. The man who had delivered it stood nearby in his smart uniform, ready to answer questions before he hopped on a train back to whence he had come.

Richenda was still lying in bed, but Hans stood, hands deep in his pockets, grinning in the morning sunshine as he watched Bertram. Eventually Bertram came up to Hans, uttered a few more "I says" and finally settled for shaking Hans firmly by the hand. It was clear that words were beyond him. I thought it, therefore, fortunate that Rory took the driver to one side and questioned him thoroughly about the workings and capabilities of the vehicle.

After a final shake, Bertram wandered off, still dazed by his good fortune, and sat in the driver's seat while things were explained to him. His expression remained puzzled until the driver hooted the horn which action, Bertram, suddenly reminiscent of a nine-year-old, repeated several times with glee. I was rather worryingly reminded of Toad from the recent children's book, *The Wind in the Willows*. Richenda had bought it for Amy and I had, with misgivings, read it to her. I feared it would only tempt her into further naughtiness.

"It is very generous of you," I said to Hans. "But I am a little afraid, not only for Bertram, but for all other users of His Majesty's roads."

Hans smiled down at me. "Bertram is doing me a very great favour escorting me to his half-brother's party. I like people to know I appreciate their help."

I put my fingers up to my neck unthinkingly, to touch the string of pearls that Hans had bestowed on me for Christmas. I knew little about jewellery, but they seemed very lovely to me. "Exactly," said Hans, watching me. Good Lord, I thought, could my pearls have cost as much as Bertram's car? I had had second thoughts about accepting such a gift, but when Richenda voiced the opinion that I might have liked something more colourful, as she would have chosen, I had quickly accepted with thanks before she could replace Hans' exquisite present with something more to her outlandish taste.

All the same, it did not seem fitting to me that my employer should give me such a costly gift. Bertram was family, and for all the Mullers' kindness to me, I was most definitely not. I could not even consider it thanks for what had happened at Christmas with Amy for, as far I knew, Rory had not been compensated in any way. I suppose Hans was now more liable to overlook his breaches of etiquette in the same way Bertram did, though I knew Hans well enough to know his ability to turn a blind eye was more limited than Bertram's. I could only hope Rory understood this or we would have a difficult time in the Highlands. Again.

To my enormous relief Bertram allowed Rory to drive. Richenda had yet, as far as I could determine, to tell Hans of her delicate state. I had, therefore, volunteered to drive up with Bertram rather than join them on the train. Susie Ellis would be accompanying them and it would give her a chance to acquaint herself at close quarters with Amy. She had only been with us two days, and already Amy had decreed that she would be called Ellie. My mother's nanny would certainly have been called by her surname, but I saw that Richenda, used to my companionship, was uncertain how to behave around Amy's new carer. This had been yet another reason not to join the Mullers in their compartment. It was high time Richenda sorted some things out for herself. She had a tendency to leave too many things to my stewardship, and while I had no strong objection to this, I could see Hans was becoming disappointed with his wife's inability to rise to her task of being mistress of the house. Perhaps after this new addition to the family, Richenda would see the wisdom of throwing herself into country life and becoming the hostess Hans would need to further his business prospects.

I climbed into the back of the automobile. Rory had the engine running. Stone loaded my baggage and I settled myself as I waited for Bertram. Despite the fact that women are presumed to be the ones who take the most time to arrange themselves for outings, I had never yet known Bertram to be on time. Rory was already at the wheel, one finger drumming against it. I knew he hated lateness. In fact, in so many ways, he must find it irritating to work for Bertram, I thought. Still, he had persisted and was now, it seemed, steward of Bertram's estate in all but name. I knew Rory was ambitious, and I assumed that when he had learned all he could in his current position he would move on. He certainly would not be short of offers: he had come to the attention of a number of significant people when he had stepped in to run the household of an Earl at short notice.[1]

There was a mirror attached near the driver's seat for rear viewing. I studied what I could of Rory in it. His face was closed, and he was frowning. His most notable feature, his vibrant green eyes, were more than half hidden by their lids. There were a few more lines on his face, frown lines in particular, and a certain grimness about him that had not been present when we first met at Stapleford Hall, when he was butler and I was a

---

[1] See my journal *A Death in the Wedding Party*.

maid.[1] He had always been of a sharp intelligence and never one to let lower-ranked servants take him for a fool, but there was a darkness now in him that worried me.

I coughed very slightly. Rory and I had reached a truce of some kind over Christmas. Perhaps now was my chance to further repair our relationship and offer what help I could. I did not like seeing him like this, but worst still, I could not think of the cause.

"Rory —" I began, when the door opened and Bertram bounced in.

"Sorry about that, chaps," he said. "I was just getting a hamper of some stuff for the journey."

"I thought you had intended to stop for lunch, sir?" said Rory, very politely.

Bertram shrugged airily. "You never know what kind of fare you are going to get further north. I thought it best to ensure we had some decent English food with us."

I groaned silently. How could Bertram have forgotten Rory was Scottish?

"Indeed, sir," replied Rory. "Black pudding and haggis are traditional fare during the Hogmanay period. It is to be hoped that Sir Richard has managed to find a decent supplier."

---

[1] I thought perhaps the grimness might be ascribed to the ever-sinking estate Bertram owned. Living in the Fens, I had found from my time there, was both beautiful and an extremely trying position. In some ways, Bertram was the least of my worries and that was saying something indeed.

"Black pudding?" said Bertram, blanching. "Isn't that made of pigs' blood?"

"And haggis out of sheep's stomach," added Rory. Then he let out the choke, or whatever it is, and we started off with a roar and a scrabbling of gravel. In the mirror, I saw a smile flicker over his face. Perhaps there were shades of the Rory I had known and loved left after all.

Once we were decently underway, and accustomed to the dull rolling noise of the road beneath the wheels, Bertram turned to me. "It's damned good you don't get — er — incommoded by automobile travel. So many ladies do!"

"Felicity?" I asked, smiling, referring to the young woman who had been the cause of Bertram's alarming adoption of facial hair. It had grown so raggedly that he had looked like a vagrant, whatever he wore. Fortunately, both Felicity and the beard had now vanished from our horizon.

"Didn't like 'em at all," said Bertram. "Should have known it would never have worked between us."

"Not to mention she was only seventeen."

"Oh come on, Euphemia, it's quite the done thing for a man of my age to wed a younger wife."

"I know," I said, imbuing the two words with as much meaning as possible. "But you are an intelligent man, and I honestly fear that a wife without equal intellect would bore you."

"At least once her charms began to fade," said Rory. "Euphemia's right. You're well out of that one."

I was close enough to see the tips of Bertram's ears go red, but he did not respond. I would have to ask Rory if he had ever had ever spoken with her and if he had formed any strong impressions. There was a short, uncomfortable silence during which I drew the conclusion that even Bertram now realised he had made something of a fool of himself over the girl. I lapsed into silence and watched the view from the window. Bertram put his head back and dozed. We drove on for long enough that my stomach was beginning to yearn for lunch.

"By the way, Euphemia, if anyone asks, you're my sister," said Bertram suddenly. He hadn't even opened his eyes.

"Are you dreaming? You cannot expect Richard Stapleford not to know his own twin. Besides, I look nothing like Richenda!" There was a muffled snort from the driver's seat and I realised Rory was trying not to laugh.

"No, no," said Bertram. "I meant if we stop on the way. McLeod thinks we can make it in one long run, but I'm not going without my lunch or supper."

"Your delicate constitution," I murmured.

Bertram shot me a dirty look. "You are well aware I do not have robust health. The doctor has advised me to keep my diet on a good footing."

"I don't think he meant you were meant to eat more," I said as kindly as I could. "In fact, Bertram, I was looking for a time to mention this delicately. How can I put this? I think your collar is growing tight."

"Damned new tailor," said Bertram, running a finger round the edge.

"Och, yer cannae blame that on the poor man. He cannae work against nature." Rory had become alarmingly Scottish again. I wondered if this meant we were nearing the border.

"I am merely concerned for your well-being. I understand that excess weight can put an extra burden on the heart."

"I think we have spoken quite too much about my heart during this trip," said Bertram from behind gritted teeth. "If there is anyone's offending organ we should be discussing it is Richard's."

The vehicle swerved suddenly, but after a heart stopping moment, Rory reclaimed control. "Whet are ye on about, man?" he asked in horrified tones.

"His heart," snapped Bertram. This time his whole face suffused with blood. "I am talking about his heart!"

"I was not aware he had one," I said.

"Well, Miss Lucinda Hessleton would not agree with you."

"Who?" asked Rory and I in unison.

Bertram's face registered surprise. "Why, his fiancée of course. I assume she thinks he has one."

"Richard's getting married?" repeated Rory and I together, sounding like a pair of bad vaudeville comedians.

"Of course. What did you think this party was all about?" asked Bertram. "Personally, I wouldn't be surprised if they tie the knot while we're there. You can do so more quickly in Scotland, I believe."

"But why?" I asked, struggling to come to terms with the concept of any sane woman agreeing to marry Richard.

Rory, his eyes still fixed on the road and his tone flat, said, "I expect it's to do with his organ."

CHAPTER
SIX

Lovely Lucinda

We had to stop the automobile so Bertram could take some air. Fortunately, we were in a rural spot and it was easy enough to pull over and find somewhere secluded. I asked Rory to unload the hamper and set about arranging an early luncheon. I hoped that food would prove a distraction to Bertram, as I carefully placed an elegant plate the cook had provided. It is a mystery to me why cooks insist on providing delicate crockery for outdoor eating, especially when it is a man who has requested the hamper. Surely, anyone who has ever known a man knows he would be perfectly happy ripping into chicken legs with his teeth and eating his meal off the grass? Though perhaps she had included the plates for me. In which case we would have only needed one, not this vast array of things that even included a teapot and tea strainer. I hid these under the cloth. It was unrealistic to think they could possibly survive an encounter with both Bertram and the outdoors.

"Are you suggesting she is pregnant?" asked Bertram.

"I never said a word!" I said, startled. "Good grief, Bertram, how on earth did you guess?"

Bertram nodded past me. I turned to see Rory standing behind me. "I was talking to him."

"Is that what you got yourself so het up about?" asked Rory. "That I was impugning the honour of your half-brother's bride to be?"

"Yes. No," spluttered Bertram. "Euphemia!"

"Ach, you mean I shouldnae have said such a thing in front of her?" Rory shuffled himself to a seated position. "Aye, well, maybe you're right. I wasnae suggesting what you thought. Rather that yon mannie would be keen to bed his bride."

"McLeod!" exploded Bertram. I offered him a sandwich. He took it without apparent thought or recognition.

"I'm sorry," said Rory. "I meant no offence, Euphemia. I didnae realise you'd become sich a lady."

I placed the plate pointedly in front of him rather than offering it to him. "Your comments, as you well know, would be out of order in front of a kitchen maid, let alone myself."

Bertram grinned. "She's got you there."

"Aye, maybe," muttered Rory, taking a sandwich and biting into it. In a rather more muffled tone, he added, "But what I want to know is how she knew the woman was pregnant."

"I thought you said she wasn't?" said Bertram, now more bemused than angry.

"I said I had no idea either way," responded Rory. "It was Euphemia that intimated she knew."

"I had no idea that Sir Richard was even contemplating matrimony," I protested. My heart sank as I realised what had happened. "Does anyone fancy some tea? There is hot water in a flask, and a teapot included in the hamper."

"Euphemia," said Bertram warningly.

"Who were ye talking about, then?" added Rory, clearly glad to be the focus of attention no longer.

There was no way I was getting out of this. "I misunderstood you, Bertram. I shouldn't have said anything. It is a secret as yet undisclosed to any other."

"You're not!" said Rory.

"Richenda," said Bertram.

I gave Rory another of my withering looks, but, really, he seemed to be growing quite impervious to them. "Yes, Richenda, but she hasn't even told Hans yet."

"Why ever not?" asked Rory.

"I thought she had gained a bit of weight," said Bertram thoughtfully. "Not the kind of thing one comments on in a woman. Especially me sister," he added with feeling. "I assume it's because Hans' last wife miscarried so frequently, she does not want to raise false hopes until she is sure."

"Goodness, Bertram," I said, "that's quite insightful."

Bertram looked a little hurt. "I can be, you know."

"Aye, well, means she'll be taking it easy. That's a good thing," said Rory. "Less chance of arguments, misunderstandings and catastrophes. Though I don't like the new nursery maid Muller's hired; something not right about her."

42

"Catastrophes," echoed Bertram. "Indeed, I hope not. Before I encountered Euphemia I had been into the realm of Scotland many times without anything disastrous befalling me."

I spluttered in indignation.

"Aye, well, let's eat up," said Rory. "Or we'll no' be there before nightfall."

Our journey continued. Bertram insisted we stopped for a proper luncheon, despite the lateness of the hour, but Rory made good time and although I had no intention of telling him so, I realised he had become most adept in controlling the automobile. We arrived outside a set of large iron lodge gates just as dusk was creeping into night.

The gates were tall and surprisingly new-looking. A small, neat lodge house stood to the left, and while this was obviously an older building, with its tiny windows and slate roof, it too looked in remarkably good repair. "I take it this is Peterfield," I said to Bertram. "It appears to be in excellent condition."

Bertram grunted. "We haven't seen the house yet, but I've heard Richard has been pouring money into the place. That new agent of his — dislikeable fellow, but knows his job."

Rory blew his horn and, within moments, the door to the lodge had opened. A bent old man shuffled out.

"Surely he would have heard the car," I said.

"He doesnae look of an age to put on a turn of speed," said Rory.

"But why would Richard . . ." I stopped. Bertram and Richard might be at odds, but they were still family and Bertram believed me to be of much lower status. It was not for me to criticise his brother's running of the estate.

"Keep him on?" finished Bertram for me. "I said his agent was a clever man. He'll know the importance of keeping the locals on side."

"Unlike at the hunting lodge," muttered Rory.

I shivered at those memories. The old man opened the gates. Bertram opened his window and tipped the man a coin. We drove on, the gravel drive spewing up dust around us. "Newly laid," muttered Rory. "Can hardly see a thing. I hope I don't drive into the house."

The drive arched away to the left and then, even above the dust clouds, we saw Peterfield.

"It's enormous," said Bertram.

In my time, I have had occasion to stay in a few of the great houses of our country and to my eye, Peterfield was no rival. As we grew closer I could see it had some age, though there seemed to be a mixture of old and new stone. The roof was clearly new. It presented a standard square face to us on approach, with a single similarly square tower rising above the wings that ran to a height of two storeys. These wings met at a place that was part house, part wall and part entrance. The actual main house was taller than the entrance, looming above it, and the opening in the front wall as we passed through it showed this section to be no more than one room wide.

I feel I am not describing the building well, and in my defence, I must say that the whole thing was a mishmash. I think I can best describe it as a building built in the style of the large castles of Scotland, such as Edinburgh, but without either the money for the full extension or the sense of grace and power. Picture a child's toy fort and you will not be far wrong. Little Joe would have loved it. Bertram was clearly overwhelmed by its faux grandeur, but in the mirror I saw Rory's upper lip curl into a sneer. For once, I quite agreed with him. The whole structure was a parody and an insult to Scotland's true castles.

"Looks like we've been sighted from the battlements," said Rory as he drove through the archway. There, standing at the top of an impressive stair, stood the unmistakable figure of Richard Stapleford. He had his arm around the waist of a slim, girlish figure. Even from a distance, we could see she was dressed in the very latest fashion. I heard Bertram's sudden intake of breath.

"Gosh," he said. "That must be Lucinda."

"I take it ye hadnae met your brother's intended?" asked Rory.

"No," said Bertram in a slightly breathless voice. "I had not."

Rory brought the car to a standstill and, first, helped Bertram and I out. Richard came down the steps with his fiancée, still gripping her around the waist. He held out a hand to Bertram, who shook it without thinking.

"My dear Euphemia, my dear Bertram," said Richard, "allow me the very great pleasure of welcoming you to my small Scottish home." He paused and turned to look at the girl. "And of introducing you to my bride-to-be, the very lovely Miss Lucinda Hessleton."

Close to, the beauty of the girl was even clearer. Her eyes were large and of the deep blue that is almost violet. Her face was heart-shaped and she smiled with apparent sweetness and sincerity.

"We are both so glad you could join us for the wedding," she said. The voice was light and pleasing, with only the slightest hint that her accent was due to elocution lessons rather than upbringing.

By now, Bertram was gulping so hard I feared that we would soon discover if it was possible for a man to swallow his own Adam's apple. "Honoured," he said, possessing himself of one of Lucinda's hands and bowing over it.

"May I call you Bertram?" asked Lucinda. "After all, I shall soon be your sister."

Even I had to acknowledge it was a well-judged comment. It was gently delivered, but reminded Bertram exactly who he was drooling over.

"Of course. Of course," said Bertram, straightening up. "Delighted."

Richard gestured to the head of the stairs, where other figures stood waiting. "Please go up. We have heard from the station that Richenda's train has arrived and they will be here any minute. Lucinda and I must stay to welcome them. My servants will make you comfortable. I believe you know my housekeeper, Mrs Lewis."

The last comment was directed at me and obviously intended to remind me of my previous employment as his maid. Or perhaps he was reminding us of Mrs Lewis' unusual appearance. I still could not look at her without remembering the gargoyles on my father's church. This was much to my shame, as I knew her to be a fair and kind woman, but more than one of the staff at Stapleford Hall had screamed on unexpectedly encountering her after dark in the house corridors.

A frown crossed Lucinda's face and she looked up at Richard, obviously puzzled by his comment. Though he kept his arm around her, Richard did not respond.

"Thank you for inviting us," I said to Lucinda. "I am very much looking forward to celebrating with you on your special day."

Lucinda blushed and, pulling away from Richard, held out her hands to me. "And I must thank you. It will be so nice to have another woman of my age to talk to. Mary is here, of course, but she can be a bit stuffy!"

Richard made a grumbling noise and she stepped back by his side. After a moment's awkwardness Bertram harrumphed, nodded at Richard and ushered me up the steps.

"Good Lord," he said in my ear as we climbed. "What is a glorious creature like that doing with my brother?" I too was surprised and confused. I could practically feel Bertram bristling with chivalric indignation.

"I am sure the young lady knows what she is doing," I said in an attempt to suppress any foolishness on Bertram's part, but in truth I felt as if I should rush to Lucinda's side and tell her of her groom's true nature. "We would not be thanked for any interference."

"Hmph!" said Bertram again.

Then Mrs Lewis was greeting us and we were caught up in being introduced to the many staff and escorted to our rooms. I went through the motions as my mother had taught me, but I could not rid myself of a strong sense of foreboding.

CHAPTER
SEVEN

Euphemia's foreboding

I had been given a room in the tower. A small fire flickered in a quaint little tiled grate. The room was surprisingly large and furnished with a four-poster bed, dressing table, two chairs, a small table and a wardrobe. There was even a sink. Other washing necessities were shared with the other bedrooms on this floor, of which there appeared to be only another two. The room and furnishings had been liberally covered with tartan. Mrs Lewis, who had herself seen me up, must have noticed my face.

"This is the blue tartan room. Quite restful to my mind." She grimaced slightly and I realised she was trying to smile. "You should see the red, yellow and green tartan rooms. They are quite something."

"I can imagine," I said with feeling. "I am grateful. Is there anything I should know about the running of events? Mr Bertram did not inform us that Sir Richard was marrying until we were underway. I fear none of us have brought gifts."

"Sir Richard wanted things this way," replied Mrs Lewis. "I do not believe any of the guests have been forewarned about the wedding. We have a local minister and the village church is very pretty and quaint. Miss Lucinda has taken quite a fancy to it."

"It certainly seems to be a very large property. Though much of it appears new?"

Mrs Lewis stiffened. "There was a fire," she said, her voice strangely flat. "The previous owners could not face restoring the property, so . . ."

"Sir Richard found himself a bargain," I said brightly. "He is a very shrewd businessman, I believe."

"Yes, miss," said Mrs Lewis, turning to leave. "The bell is there if you need anything. It does take the maids a few minutes to reach this level, but we are more than adequately staffed to fulfil all our guests' needs. Dinner tonight will be a formal affair in the Great Hall. I believe Sir Richard will announce the schedule for the visit then. Drinks before in the Red Salon. If you come straight down the stairs there will be a footman at the bottom to direct you."

With that, she was gone. Only a few moments later a maid knocked on my door and asked to unpack for me. I allowed her to do so and asked that a dark blue dress might be pressed for me to wear for dinner.

"I could also do with a cup of tea," I said. "We have been travelling for such a long time. Perhaps you could manage them both at once, if you were careful?"

The maid, who I judged to be no more than sixteen, freckled and with the flaming red hair that is only found north of the English border, bobbed a little curtsey. "That's nice of you, miss, but we're all used to running up and down the stairs. Keeps ye trim! So don't be worried about pulling the bell. I'm here to help!"

"I see . . . ?"

"Enid, miss."

"Thank you, Enid. Are Mr and Mrs Muller on this level too?"

"No, miss. They've been put on the other side, so they can be nearer the nursery for their daughter. It's Miss Hessleton on this level, along with her friend Miss Grantham. But don't worry about getting lost. There'll be footmen patrolling the corridors to direct people."

"Surely not on the ladies' floor!"

"Well, no, miss. But one will be in the hall, at the bottom of the stairs. And ye've got the bell. Sir Richard has thought of everything. He's done the place up right nice." She then blushed furiously and bowed her head. "Sorry, miss. Mrs Lewis is always scolding me for being too familiar."

I dismissed this comment with a wave of my hand. "So you find Sir Richard to be a good master?" I asked.

Enid looked back up at me, her eyes shining like stars. "Och, the very best, miss."

Later, I made my way down the stairs. They were uncarpeted stone, but each tread had been carefully restored. The result was authentic — and cold; much as I imagine a real castle to be. At the bottom a man dressed in livery bowed and escorted me to a pair of double doors, which he opened to reveal the Red Salon. There was already a crowd of perhaps twenty or more people standing around with drinks in their hands. I nodded to the room as I entered and made my way across towards where the drinks were being dispensed by yet another footman. This room was large, square, and fitted out with dark panelling, and carpeted in a shade all too close to the colour of blood. The ceiling was ornately plastered with images I could not study without craning my neck and looking like a lost giraffe. A row of tall windows looked out not onto the courtyard, but onto a misty vista of green hills with the shadows of what I assumed must be mountains beyond. At one end, a large fireplace, taller than I, roared as it consumed a couple of tree-like logs. Despite this, and the number of guests, the room still felt cold.

Suddenly, a drink was pressed into my hand. Bertram's voice spoke into my ear. "I know things up here come a lot cheaper, but how the hell is my brother affording all this?"

It was a question that, as a lady, I should have ignored, but my interest too had been piqued. "I have no idea," I whispered back. "And who is Miss Hessleton? You knew about the marriage. What do you know of the bride?"

"Family comes from trade," said Bertram darkly. "Mills and the like. Perhaps Richard had a down payment on the dowry?"

I warred inwardly for a moment with my mother's ruling against gossip, but gave in. "If she is that rich, surely they could have got her someone with a more important title? There are many great houses who would welcome a rich bride."

"But with a mother who had been a servant?" countered Bertram.

"Oh," I said.

"Besides, I believe there is also a son up at Cambridge who wants to enter politics. No use, of course. You need to be an Oxford man to get anywhere."

I smiled. "I assume you were an Oxford man?"

"Rowing Blue," said Bertram with pride. Then his face fell. "That was before I started getting trouble with the old ticker."

"Well, let us hope that this trip into the Kingdom's northern realm will provide you with some rest and relaxation."

"If it hadn't been for Hans . . ." Bertram trailed off, but then added, "Apart from Amy trying to fall off the roof, we had a rather good Christmas, didn't we?"

My heart went out to him. All the Stapleford children had been neglected by their parents, and none had known the happy Christmases that I had enjoyed with my parents and little brother. Richenda would not countenance my going home to share Christmas with my mother and little Joe, but at least I had many happy memories. "Actually," I said, "it was rather nice, wasn't it?"

"And no one died," said Bertram, with a wicked grin.

"Don't say things like that, Bertram," I said.

"You think I am tempting fate?"

"I hope to the Good Lord not," I said, but even as I spoke I felt a ghost pass over my grave. I shivered, and urged Bertram to move closer to the fire. But despite the roaring flames, the feeling of cold had settled into my bones.

CHAPTER
EIGHT

An MP with a castle — and a fortune

I was taken into dinner by the most boring of men — an ageing financier, who was full of bluster about the incomprehensible deals he had done in his youth. On my other side sat the youngest of nine sons of a Scottish Lord, who was clearly uncomfortable about the formality with which Richard was conducting the meal. It has often seemed to me that the newly rich try much harder than established families do when it comes to formal dining. The old brigade do it all without conscious effort, whereas everything Richard did was with flourish and too much silver and gold plate. Not, I should hasten to add, that I am particularly fond of the aristocracy. Until recently, my closest companions have been among the servant class, who I have found much more honest, decent and hardworking than their employers.

The meal wore on; course after course. I lost count after seven. I could see that even Bertram, who was seated some way down the table on the opposite side, was beginning to struggle with the amount of food he was expected to consume. Adopting the woman's prerogative, I ate only mouthfuls of each course. I abhorred the waste of food, but it was either that or I would have to ask Enid to cut me out of my dress that night.

Finally, we were getting to the stage when the ladies could expect to retire while the gentlemen drank their port. It was also my chance to slip away to my room for an early night. Bertram would doubtless drink port into the early hours if his host allowed, and apart from Richenda there was really no one I would want to converse with. Of course, I was a companion and would have to take my lead from my employer, but hopefully the journey, coupled with her interesting condition, would make her head for bed.

I cast about trying to work out who the highest ranking lady present was, but having removed myself from society — or rather my mother having rather spectacularly removed herself from the upper echelons by her youthful folly of marrying my father — I could only identify a few of the women present. I did remark that Lucinda positively glowed with happiness. On more than one occasion, I saw her cast admiring glances at her groom-to-be. As far as I could tell these were sincere. Never before had the adage that beauty is in the eye of the beholder seemed more apt to me.

However, it was not a lady who rose but Sir Richard himself. He tapped his knife lightly on the side of his crystal glass and called for silence. "It seems," he began, "that the cat is out of the bag and that many of you have discovered, one way or another," — he paused to give his audience what I assume was meant to be a comic look. I shuddered — "that this New Year's celebration is more than a little gathering to mark my engagement, but you will also all be guests at my wedding on New Year's Day when I have the good fortune to marry Miss Lucinda Hessleton."

Whatever he was going to say next was lost in a round of applause and cheers; some men present, who had obviously enjoyed the wine too well, went as far as to bang their forks on the table. Eventually Sir Richard managed to hush the crowd and continue. "Now, this might appear to be unseemly haste, but ladies and gentlemen, while my darling bride-to-be is in the first blush of youth, I am not so fortunate." He reached out to take Lucinda's hand. "Once I had found her, I did not wish to waste a precious moment before I took her as my wife. I want our association to be as long as possible."

"And as fertile!" heckled a man's voice from further down the table.

Lucinda turned a fiery red. I saw Richard hesitate, but then he seemed to decide to take it as a joke. He kissed Lucinda's hand. "I have no doubt I will have many happy years of fatherhood to look forward to, but first my bride must have her day. When I told her of my Scottish castle, then nowhere else would do for her wedding, and as you were all already coming up for New Year — well, the rest as they say is history."

There was more applause and some positive braying, from those who I could only assume were Richard's fellow financiers rather than the more elite members of society.[1]

"Gentlemen, gentlemen," cried Richard over the racket. "As my wife-to-be wishes for a Highland wedding, upon your return to your rooms you will all find I have supplied a Highland rig out. The ladies, of course, will no doubt look charming in whatever they intended to wear for New Year. Until then, please feel free to enjoy the facilities of my estate. My servants will be arranging whist and bridge leagues for the ladies. My gillies will be happy to escort any who take a fancy to see our lovely glen. There will be, my cook promises, glorious meals. My mother-in-law is keen to put on a play, should any be inclined to indulge her. There is a well-stocked library, a billiards room, a flower room and much more. Simply ask for whatever you seek and my servants will be happy to supply it. Over the coming three days Lucinda and I will endeavour to spend time with all of you individually, welcoming you to our home. Our hope is that in the run-up to our wedding you will have a relaxing and luxurious three days, before, in the New Year, we all return to the business of our everyday lives." He paused. "Well, not I," he said, "for Lucinda and I are off on a romantic tour." Then he put his finger to his lips and said, in what I assume he thought was a coy fashion, but one I found merely lecherous, "not that the young lady is allowed to know the surprises I have in store for her!"

---

[1] Though after enough wine it seems to me that most men forget what class they spring from.

There were positive shouts of enthusiasm at the end of this remark. Fortunately, as I was by now feeling distinctly queasy, one of the older matrons, all dark colours and diamond jewels, rose, and all the ladies followed suit. She hesitated and I realised she had no more idea than the rest of us where the Withdrawing Room was. A footman opened the door to usher us forward and the redoubtable lady marched out with her head held high. There was a general scraping of chairs as the gentlemen stood and the ladies made their way out of the room. It was distinctly disorganised, and clearly showed that the people present were not all of the same set.

I was peering around trying to pick out Richenda in the general exodus, when a footman came up to me. He was well over six foot and had to bend low to address me. "Miss St John?" I nodded. "Sir Richard has asked that you join him and the rest of the family in the Stuart Room in fifteen minutes. I am instructed to escort you."

There appeared to be no way to decline this invitation. There was nothing inappropriate in the man's behaviour, but he was tall and broad enough to exert a commanding presence. "Are you sure they want me at a family meeting?" I asked in a half-hearted attempt to get away.

"Indeed, ma'am. I was asked most specifically to reassure you that your presence is greatly desired."

I sighed inwardly and gestured to him to lead on. Over the next few minutes, I was conducted along a confusing mishmash of corridors and vaulted passageways. I tried hard to keep track of the route we were taking, but after the fifth turn I was too dizzy trying to work out in which area of the castle we now were. The footman must have noticed my confusion. "Please don't be concerned, ma'am. Being a mixture of the old and the new, the castle is a confusing place for guests. Sir Richard has ensured that there are to be servants on watch day and night to help conduct the ladies and gentlemen until they get their bearings."

"I don't know that I ever will," I said candidly. "I have no idea how you remember the way . . ."

"Rupert, ma'am," responded the footman, "I have the advantage of having worked previously at the old castle, so I have only had to memorise the new buildings, and they, if I might say so, are quite straightforward in comparison to the older remnants."

"What happened to the old castle?"

"An unfortunate fire, ma'am, but please, have no fear. Sir Richard has put in place the most modern of safety features."

"That must have been quite a fire to destroy so much," I said. "How terrifying. I do hope no one was injured."

"We are here, ma'am," said Rupert, his hand placed on the door handle. He gave a little cough. "I fear I have spoken too freely. Sir Richard does not like to be reminded of how he acquired the castle. Miss Lucinda is afraid of ghosts and he does not wish her to hear any stories. And, well, it is still a source of distress to the local people. We are all most grateful to Sir Richard for acquiring and modernising the castle. It has always been the main provider for the livelihoods of the local people."

I saw real fear in his eyes, and realised that the staff were perhaps beginning to get the measure of how ruthless Richard could be. "I won't say a word," I said.

Then he opened the door and I stepped into a smaller, comfortably furnished salon with a fire blazing and a tea set out on a table by a window. Otherwise, the room was empty. I moved towards the window in an attempt to peer behind the drawn curtains and get my bearings. As I did so, I heard the door click shut behind me as Rupert departed. The vista before me held nothing but blackness and the reflected images of the room. I let the curtain drop again and, feeling suddenly cold, I went to stand by the fire. Inside my head, a small voice whispered that it had not been wise to agree to go off alone in Richard Stapleford's castle. We had been adversaries for a long time and I had no doubt he would take any revenge that chance offered him. I eyed the silver sugar tongs, wondering if they could be used as a weapon. Doubtless Fitzroy, the spy I had the strange habit of encountering, could have used them to deadly effect, but I doubted I could give anyone more than a bad pinch. Still, anything was better than nothing.

My fingers had barely closed around the tongs when the door burst open and my worst fears were realised. Sir Richard Stapleford strode into the room. "Euphemia! At last!" he said, and gave me a smile that chilled me to the marrow.

CHAPTER
NINE

The Staplefords squabble

My fear was short-lived as Lucinda tripped into the room behind him. She ran over and embraced me, kissing me on both cheeks. "I know how important you are to Richard's family," she said. "And that you are to be treated as family, yourself."

I looked across her, for she was some inches smaller than me at the head of the family. He merely beamed at me. I immediately regretted eating so much for dinner, as my stomach lurched in disgust. "How kind," I murmured to Lucinda.

"I am afraid my bridesmaids are already chosen," said Lucinda, "but I have been trying to think of a special role for you in the ceremony."

"There really is no need," I protested. From the look on Richard's face, he was enjoying my discomfort. Lucinda drew me over to a pair of chairs by the fire, chatting earnestly about her wedding plans and how I might be included. I only lent her half an ear. Firstly, because I was determined not to get involved in the ceremony, and secondly, because with an eagerness befitting a bride about to be married, she was bursting with far too many details and schemes.

"Mummy and Daddy send their apologies, but they are early retirees. They hope to meet you at breakfast."

I smiled at her and let her ramble on. I did not have the heart to openly quash her plans. She seemed an eager little thing, keen to please and very friendly. There was no sign of malicious intent in her plans or her manner, something one would have expected to find in Richard's true soulmate. All in all, she seemed a pretty, friendly, ordinary girl. As she was only interested in talking about the wedding it was difficult for me to assess her intellect, but as she had chosen Richard as a life mate I could only assume she was either mentally challenged or extremely naïve. I had certainly been ready to dislike Richard's intended, but it was like trying to dislike a playful and appealing puppy.

Fortunately, it was not long before Bertram, Hans and Richenda joined us. Richenda burst into the room, saying, "I hope this will not take long, Richard. This is the first night Amy has spent away from home and I want to see her settled."

"Haven't you got my sister a nursery maid, Muller?" demanded Richard. "I don't know how your parents did things, but my sister and I were raised by servants in the correct manner. Bertram's mother tried to interfere a mite too much when he was in the nursery, but our father soon put a stop to that. You can't mollycoddle children if you want them to have any moral fibre."

"Good God!" exploded Bertram. "I don't know which part of that speech I object to most. You speaking about moral fibre? Ridiculous!"

"My wife has all the servants she requires," said Hans in an obviously controlled voice. I knew him well enough now to know when he was using his preternatural aura of calm.

"Honestly, Richard, you are being abominably rude," exclaimed Richenda. "I thought this gathering was all about mending bridges and trying to be a family. All you are doing is reminding me why I left Stapleford Hall in the first place. I pity your poor bride. She seemed harmless enough. I assume she doesn't know you very well, and that she is a trade heiress. Slightly better than going for an American, but it's really a pretty poor show, brother. It's not as if you weren't already rolling in the stuff."

"Richenda!" said Hans shortly. He gave her a look that caused Richenda to blush fiery red.

At this point Lucinda stood up and came forward. As I saw the expression on Richenda's face, I realised that Richard had been blocking her view of the slight girl. "Thank you so much for coming to our wedding," said Lucinda in a gentle voice. "I too am hoping that we can all become a happy family." She turned to her fiancée, "Richard, I do think you could have postponed any family reunion until tomorrow. The others must be tired after their long journey. And I quite understand about Amy," she added, turning back to Richenda. "I have a little cousin who sometimes comes to stay with Mummy and Daddy, and though she has been coming for the past three years, she is always a little unsettled on the first night. Poor Amy! First night away from home in an enormous place like this! But I am sure you have chosen an excellent nanny. Richard has spoken of how devoted you are to your daughter."

"Adopted daughter," corrected Richard.

"Richenda's concern makes it very clear, darling, that she considers Amy as her own blood," said Lucinda. "And why not? I think it was a totally splendid thing of you and your husband to take her in."

Richenda went an even deeper shade of crimson and muttered something about Lucinda being very kind. Hans watched Richard's bride-to-be with a puzzled expression on his face. Bertram was wide-eyed and slack-jawed. I felt unaccountably annoyed with him.

Richard placed a protective hand on Lucinda's shoulder. "It matters, my dear, because the first of us to have a legitimate child inherits the family seat at Stapleford Hall." He smiled down at her. "Something I am very much hoping you will help me do."

It was Lucinda's turn to blush now, her radiant skin flushing a slightly rose-tinted hue. If anything, she looked lovely, and could not have made a worse — or better — contrast to poor Richenda's ruddy complexion. I wondered if Bertram was about to start drooling again, but he managed to shut his jaw and mutter, "Some things one doesn't talk about in front of ladies."

Richard went over to the drinks table and poured scotch for the men. Lucinda invited Richenda and I to join her in sitting by the fire, where she stared rather helplessly at the tea tray until Richenda took charge. Lucinda chattered on, but I barely heard her. Richenda's face revealed a torrent of emotions stirring inside her. I tried to catch her eye. My stomach was churning. I feared all too well what she was about to do.

Richenda smoothed down her skirts, took a deep breath, and said, "Actually, Richard, I think you'll find Stapleford Hall will become mine." She smiled widely and patted her stomach. "You see, I am already with child."

CHAPTER
TEN

A severe attack of chivalry

There is an expression "then all hell broke loose", and this would not be an incorrect way of describing what followed Richenda's announcement.

Hans threw himself to the floor at her feet, begging her to tell him if this was really true. Bertram choked on his scotch. Richard bellowed, "Damn you, sister, this had better not be true or I'll have your hide!" Lucinda fainted neatly onto the sofa, unnoticed by everyone but me.

Hans sprang to his feet and stood, fists clenched at his sides, in front of Richard. "How dare you address my wife in such a manner!" he cried in an emotion-filled voice that was very unlike him.

"Congratulations, sis!" said Bertram, attempting to calm the situation. "Jolly well done, old chap," he said to Hans, tugging at his sleeve and attempting to defuse his confrontation with Richard.

But it was Richard who broke away first, brushing rudely past Hans. "You know I will have my way, Richenda!" he flung over his shoulder as he stormed out of the door. He slammed it behind him and, despite us being in a stone room, I swear I almost felt the walls shudder.

"Richenda, you should have told me," said Hans. "I would never have brought you up here if I had known."

"Don't see you would have had much choice," said Bertram. "What with all the work on the house."

"What work?" asked Richenda.

Hans threw Bertram a cross look. "It was meant as a surprise. I am having the house converted to electricity. I am assured it is a much safer system than gas, and with a child in the house —" he swallowed and corrected himself, "with children in the house it was the best course of action." Then he took both her hands in his and kissed them passionately. Bertram coughed uncomfortably, tried to kick a log on the fire and almost fell in.

"I hate to mention it," I said, "but I think Lucinda did not faint out of etiquette. She is out cold." I slapped her hands. "She's not coming to."

"Oh Lord," said Bertram, and rang the bell.

"Probably the first time she's seen Richard's true colours. Bound to be a shock for the gal," said Richenda, but her gaze did not leave Hans' face. "You are pleased, aren't you?" she asked him. "I'm so sorry I didn't tell you before, but after speaking with the doctor today I wanted to wait a little longer until . . ."

"I understand," said Hans thickly, and kissed her hands once more.

Bertram grimaced. "If you don't mind, old chap, I've had rather a lot to eat tonight and that's a bit much to stomach."

"Of course," said Hans. He raised Richenda to her feet. "We will leave you. My wife and I have much to discuss." His eyes rested fondly on her. "My dearest wife, my darling Richenda . . ."

"Oh Lord!" said Bertram. Hans and Richenda left the room, practically floating on a cloud. Bertram edged towards the door.

"Oh no you don't," I said. "We have to do something about Lucinda."

"I rang the bell," protested Bertram. "You can't really expect more from a man in situations like these."

"But no one has come."

"I could ring it again," said Bertram.

"What an excellent idea."

He did so. We waited. "Do you think scotch might help?" I asked.

"Good idea," said Bertram, and poured himself another.

"That wasn't what I meant," I began when the door opened and a footman entered, followed by an older woman dressed in a maid's uniform, who rushed to Lucinda's side and held a little bottle under her nose. The stench of ammonia drifted towards me and I rose to stand by Bertram. Lucinda's eyelids fluttered and she gave a little moan. I could not help but notice that she moaned rather nicely, like a kitten. (Really, I had to stop thinking of her as some kind of pet — but the metaphor seemed all too apt.)

"Sir Richard has asked me to see the lady and her maid to her room," said the footman, loftily.

"Can you stand, my love?" asked the maid with alarming familiarity. "Or shall I ask this man to carry you?"

I felt Bertram draw back behind me. "She means the footman," I whispered to him.

"If I could lean on you a little, Louise," said Lucinda, as the maid helped her rise. "Has Mary retired for the night? I could do with the counsel."

"I'll get the man to find out for you, my love," said the maid. "You, Scotchman, find out if Miss Mary Hill has retired yet, and if she has not, request her to join Miss Lucinda in her rooms."

The footman gave her a look filled with disdain, but nodded curtly. The maid threw Bertram and me a furious look and helped Lucinda out of the door.

"I say," said Bertram, "that was jolly well out of order."

"Which bit?" I asked distractedly.

"That maid! The way she looked at us. Like it was all our fault."

"What else was she to think?" I replied. "We were the only two left in the room. You don't think it could be the same Mary Hill, do you?"

"Same?" asked Bertram. Then realisation dawned in his eyes. For all Bertram can, far too frequently, and especially around his family, perform an excellent impression of an idiot, he has a quick and active mind. "Mary Hill, the suffragette, who you were in jail with and who you wrongly accused of murder?"

"We accused," I said automatically.

"It was your idea to do the confrontational tea."

"Confrontational tea! What a way of putting it." I sighed and rubbed a hand across my tired eyes. "But

69

yes, you're right. Really, this New Year is getting better and better."

"Never mind," said Bertram, patting me on the shoulder awkwardly. "At least no one is dead."

"Yet."

"Don't. Just don't, Euphemia," warned Bertram.

"Do you honestly think Richard is going to sit by and let his sister take the country seat from him?"

"He doesn't need it. He's got all this! And probably more."

"It's never been about the money," I said. "Owning Stapleford Hall is an obsession with him. He killed twice to get his seat in Parliament."

"I say, hush," said Bertram. "You can't go around saying things like that. Nothing was ever proved against him."

"There's only us here," I said. "And you know it's true. Or do you think we have been misjudging your half-brother all these years?"

Bertram sat down in a wing-backed chair. "No," he said, sighing deeply. "My half-brother is as black-hearted as they come."

"The question is whether he is black-hearted, as you so poetically phrased it, enough to kill his pregnant twin sister?"

Bertram made a gargling noise and went rather pale.

"You have developed the most alarming habit of letting your jaw go slack when you are startled," I said. "It is most unattractive and makes you look quite stupid."

"Since you have become Richenda's companion," snapped Bertram, "you, Euphemia, have changed a lot and not, I may add, in a good way. When I think of the sweet little maid I first found searching my room . . ."

"That's better," I said. "You think so much better when you're annoyed than when you are startled."

Bertram raised his eyebrows at me and poured himself another scotch. "Do you really think he would murder Richenda?" he asked, taking his seat by the fire and motioning me to join him.

"I don't know," I said slowly. "It would be difficult to do. I mean, there are a lot of people in the castle and once she has returned to the Muller estate I am sure Hans can keep her safe."

"You put a lot of trust in Muller," said Bertram grumpily.

"However, it occurs to me that in a crowded castle with so many alterations, twisting staircases . . ."

"He might find her alone and off her?" finished Bertram dramatically.

"No, but he might arrange for a slight accident."

"How would that help him?" asked Bertram.

"I meant a fall."

Bertram shrugged. "I don't see how getting her bruised would help him. He's always been the kind of mean little sneak that would put trip wires across stairs when we were kids. I remember once when he got Mrs . . ." he began to giggle. "All thin gangly legs and petticoats, she was coming down the stairs. Never seen anything like it. For ages afterwards I was convinced all women were half spider —"

"I meant," I said, cutting him off, "that a fall could bring on a miscarriage." I looked at his uncomprehending expression. "Not a missed carriage, Bertram, but a miscarriage of the baby. She could lose the baby."

Bertram paled. "My God, think what that would do to Muller! After his first wife lost all those . . ."

"I do not think it would be good for Richenda, either," I said waspishly.

"No. No. Bad all round." He stood up. "Right, there is only one thing for it."

"It would be difficult to leave," I said. "We have no proof that Richard will do such a thing, and I recall that Hans needed to be here for business reasons."

"Muller knows full well what kind of man my brother is," said Bertram. "But I didn't mean that. Cause an awful fuss. No, what I meant was that you and I, Euphemia, shall have to guard my sister and her unborn child with our lives!"

CHAPTER
ELEVEN

A midnight tryst

I realised that this was the many glasses of wine Bertram had imbibed during dinner talking. "I completely understand that you wish to protect your sister," I said. "But we are not of the same ilk as someone who might make a decent protector."

"Who better than her own kith and kin?" stormed Bertram.

"Well, we know Rory is handy in a fight. But someone like Fitzroy would be better. I don't suppose he is here? He has a habit of turning up when one least expects him."

"That bounder!" exclaimed Bertram. "I'd not trust him further than I could throw him." He looked me in the eye. "Not, I admit, that that would be very far. You are right that I am not exactly a man of action — thanks largely to my dicky heart — but I have my wits about me."

"Yes, you do," I said more gently. "I suppose we must go and apprise Hans of our fears."

Bertram pulled a face. "I suppose we must, but the way he and Richenda were going on . . ." He took a deep pull from his glass. "It was quite revolting. I can only imagine what they are . . ."

"Let's not," I said hastily. "Why do you not seek out Rory and ask him to stand guard by their rooms tonight?"

A sly smile spread over Bertram's face. "He's probably relaxing in the servants' hall; flirting with the maids."

"What is it with you two?" I asked. "You have the strangest master-servant relationship I have ever encountered."

"Pot. Kettle," said Bertram. "We can reconvene after breakfast. I will meet you at the Mullers' room tomorrow at nine a.m. On second thoughts, let's make that ten a.m. I'll go set Rory to it." So saying he rose, put down his glass and wandered off, whistling tunelessly. I watched this, wondering if he had drunk even more than I had thought. Could I really trust him to find Rory and set him to watch Richenda? To convince him that it was necessary, even? For one dreadful moment, I found myself deeply missing Fitzroy.

I made my way up to my room. To my surprise, I found it quite easily. The layout of the modern side of the castle was actually far simpler than I had thought. There were more floors, but they were generally smaller than those in the old section, and were connected with direct passageways and stairs.

When I arrived in my room, I was delighted to see that Enid had been in already to lay my fire. Although the castle had been wired for electricity, Enid had lit a number of candles around the room, which gave it a warm and homely glow. I was glad of this. The new lighting system made me uneasy, and I was not looking forward to having to deal with it daily at the Muller estate — whatever Hans had said about its safety.

I could have pulled the bell to ask for her help in undressing, but as I was quite adept at this myself — as I was in styling my own hair, a skill my mother had forbidden me from ever mentioning — I got myself ready for bed, climbed under the covers (which the efficient Enid had heated with a warming pan), and blew out my candle.

At once, I was overcome with a feeling of foreboding. The room seemed to expand in the darkness. I became aware of the wind howling outside my window. Even the crackle from the fire seemed filled with a venomous menace. Although my father had been a vicar, and I had strong feelings that the preternatural and supernatural should stay quite separate from my world, I had in my previous exploits succumbed more to a belief in superstition than I would have liked.

The light of the fire ensured the room was not completely dark: instead it sent shadows dancing across the walls. I found myself checking them to be sure that they did not conceal another person. I plumped up my pillows and told myself to be rational. I had no feeling that someone was in the room with me — and as this had happened before, that in itself was reassuring — but yet my fear would not leave me. Of course, the circumstances that awaited me tomorrow — and my all-too-close involvement with the Stapleford family — would make for an uneasy time, but did I really think Richard would commit murder just before his wedding?

Were my instincts warning me that death was about to enter my life yet again? I comforted myself that Richard, however evil his intentions, was not a quick thinker, though he was cunning. He had the sense to plan rather than act rashly. I consoled myself there was likely to be no immediate threat. And yet the unease lingered.

Lucinda was a puzzle to me. That anyone should link their life willingly with Richard Stapleford's confused me, but she had appeared to be without guile. Either she was a consummate actress, or her fainting had been the result of her seeing for the first time the true nature of her husband-to-be. Were my instincts trying to tell me she was also in danger?

And Mary Hill — here? What if it was her? She had a fine mind, but she despised me. How could I draw her into my plans?

The thoughts went round and round in my head, but I could make no sense of them. I was on the verge of sleep when there was a sharp knock at my door. Instinctively, I grabbed at the nearest heavy object to hand — my unlit candlestick. I sat there, my heart beating furiously, waiting for whatever would happen next. There was another loud knock. Through my sleep-addled mind I realised that a would-be assailant would be unlikely to ask for entry. With a huge sigh, I threw back my warm and cosy covers. I could not have been lying there long as the fire still burned brightly. A third knock caused me to call out, "A moment!" while I struggled into my wrap and slipped shoes onto my feet. There was a very small part of me that wondered if it might be Rory; I own to both a slight disappointment as well as an unwelcome shock when I opened the door, and beheld the face flickering in the candlelight to be that of Mary Hill.

"This is not my idea," she said bluntly. "At least not wholly my idea, but it seems you are the only person who might be able to help me."

"Could not this discussion wait for daylight? Breakfast?" I asked wearily.

"No, it could not. I only have Lucinda's word that she will wait for my return."

I looked at her blankly. "She is threatening to run away into the night," said Mary. "It appears something happened tonight in your presence that distressed her very much."

"I hardly spoke to her!" I objected.

"No, no," snapped Mary. "I am not suggesting *you* did anything. I understand it was Sir Richard's behaviour that was to blame. She is now saying she will not marry a monster. I need you to come and convince her that Sir Richard will make a good bridegroom."

I swallowed. "I really do not think you have the right person," I said.

"I can hardly ask his sister. I believe it was their conflict that agitated the whole situation."

"I am surprised that you would urge a young woman into an arrangement she now regrets making. You are still a member of the Sisterhood, are you not?"

Even by the candlelight, I could see Mary's face darken. "Things are not always as simple as one would wish," she said. "Will you come or not?"

I hesitated. "I cannot think that giving Lucinda my opinion of Sir Richard will help," I said baldly.

"Well, if you will not help I shall have to have Sir Richard's servants rouse him to attempt to make amends."

"Surely her parents can help? And forgive me, but what business is this of yours?"

"Lucinda is my cousin on my mother's side. As for her parents, neither of them is in good health and I would rather not distress them."

A great many retorts came to mind, but I only said, "I will come, but I am not sure my intervention will secure the outcome you wish."

"Her circumstances may make you change your mind," said Mary cryptically. She then refused to answer further questions and I had no choice but to follow her bobbing candle light along the passage.

As I had been told, Lucinda's bedroom was on the same level as my own, so we managed to reach her room without the interference of any servants. At her door, Mary halted. "I want you, on your honour, to promise me you will not advise my cousin ill for your own purposes, and that you will tell her nothing but what you know to be true. I have seen before how you can fantasise the truth."

Anger and shame boiled inside my chest. Reason told me that Mary had little reason to believe in me after I had wrongly accused her of murder but, likewise, she had no knowledge of the number of issues I had resolved correctly, especially those in the service of

King and Country. "I promise," I said through gritted teeth.

Mary waited a moment more, as if deciding if she could trust my word, and then opened the door. Lying in front of the fire, on the most beautiful Persian rug, was the violently sobbing figure of Lucinda. At our entrance, she sat up, tears streaming down her beautiful face, her blue eyes brimming with more — I noted that unlike Richenda, this was a female who could cry to advantage — and reached out a hand to me melodramatically.

"At last," she cried, "Someone who will tell me the truth."

CHAPTER
TWELVE

Lucinda sees sense

I managed to get Lucinda to stop crying and sit in a chair, by dint of refusing to speak to her until she stopped her "dreadful noise."[1]

Lucinda was now hiccupping softly like a puppy that has gobbled down one too many biscuits. My initial impression that she was interested in little beyond the details of her wedding was confirmed at the sudden onslaught of tears when she suddenly said, "Now I will never wear my dress, and it suits me so well."

I heard Mary sigh beside me and for once felt completely in sympathy. "What exactly is it that distresses you, Lucinda?" I asked.

"Richard is a monster," she said, her eyes widening. "You saw how his face became reddened and he roared. He looked positively inhuman."

"He was upset," I said. "Stapleford Hall has long been a bitter bone of contention within his family."

"So he only wants me so he can own the Hall?" asked Lucinda.

My tongue tied itself into knots. Unexpectedly, Mary came to my rescue. "Lucy, you know full well that the

---

[1] I felt most uncomfortably like my mother saying this.

purpose of marriage is to ensure heirs. If this is what you are now quailing at, can I remind you that your other options are at least equally unappealing."

Lucinda nodded slowly. "And he does have a castle." Her face puckered. "But so did the ogre in the tale of the golden goose."

I turned to Mary. "Does your cousin believe Richard is literally inhuman and not as a metaphor?" I asked incredulously.

Mary shrugged. "Lucy has a lively imagination — but I cannot imagine that you believe the man to be a fairy tale monster!" she said, turning to her cousin. "That is beyond melodrama, even for you."

"Well, maybe not," admitted Lucinda, sniffing. "But you have to agree, Euphemia, he did seem quite ferocious."

"He did," I admitted, "but, as I have explained, his ire was not directed at you." I paused, but could not help myself from asking, "Has he ever shown you this side of him before? I presume you have spent some degree of time in his company?"

"Oh yes," said Lucinda. "It was a full three weeks before he proposed. It normally takes gentlemen far less time."

"So you have other suitors?" I enquired. Mary threw me a warning look.

"Oh yes, loads," said Lucinda simply. "But Mummy and Daddy have only approved of one other alongside Sir Richard, and I could not marry him!" Her eyes filled with tears once more.

"And why is this?" I asked, suppressing a yelp as Mary jabbed me in the ribs with her elbow.

"He has whiskers growing out of his nose!"

"Lucy is referring to my uncle's partner, Mr George Smythe. He is a family friend. He and my uncle were at school together."

I digested this slowly. From the glimpse I had caught of them, Lucinda's parents had seemed at an advanced age to have such a young daughter. Mary met my eyes and nodded slightly. "Lucy is the youngest of eight children. None of the others survived infancy. She is quite the miracle for her parents."

"Not as important as Pa's business," said Lucinda sadly. "It's all about the factories. Pa doesn't want his lifetime's work all broken up. He's afraid that any of the young men who have proposed might have some new-fangled idea of changing the way the business is run. He says it is his legacy."

"Mills," said Mary shortly. "They could well do with improvement, but my uncle is a traditionalist."

"That's why he likes Richard. He has promised Pa he won't change the mills one bit, and he has already signed a document leaving them in their entirety to my first son."

"Unborn son," corrected Mary.

"You are . . .?"

"No, of course she isn't," snapped Mary. "I only meant to make it clear Lucy has not been previously married."

I looked at her curiously. It seemed to me there was another story here that I was not being told. "Forgive me," I said to Lucinda, "if your father's business is entailed on your son — if entailed is the right word — what does Sir Richard gain from marrying you?"

"Me," said Lucinda, her expression puzzled.

"There is a significant amount of money in bonds and shares that her father is endowing to her," said Mary.

"There is?" asked Lucinda. "He has never mentioned it to me. Richard says he is in love with me."

I struggled to imagine Richard Stapleford in any kind of lover-like situation. The effort made me shudder in revulsion.

"You do not believe he was telling the truth?" Lucinda asked.

"I have no idea," I said.

"But you do know," interjected Mary, "that should Lucinda refuse to marry either Richard or Mr Smythe and run away into the night, it will not have a happy ending."

"Well, no. I could not advise that as a course of action. Unless perhaps there was an elopement planned?" Mary jabbed me in the ribs again.

"Well, I suppose I could ask Mr Roper if he would elope with me. He owns the chemists in the High Street. He is tall and has magnificent hair." She dropped her voice. "Mr Smythe has no hair upon his head at all!"

"Has he proposed?" I asked.

"Lucinda has had no proposals except those which her father has approved. She has been kept extremely sheltered due to her frailty."

I looked at the vision of loveliness and health before me. "Remember her deceased siblings," said Mary *sotto voce*. "Her parents have always feared for her. They are ageing and seek to have her well established and protected."

I began to see why doting parents might think a peer of the realm, rich in his own right, who was also an MP and who shared Lucinda's father's business sensibilities, might appeal. "This is dreadful," I said to Mary, my voice low.

"If anything about your membership of the Women's Movement was real," answered Mary equally quietly, "you will know that Lucinda has no money or rights. Her father owns her and may give her to whatever man he wishes. When she is married, she will then be owned by her husband and bound to his will. It is against this we must fight as for girls like Lucy, it is reality. She does not inherit the mills or her father's money. It is all made over to her first son and, for now, there is no way of circumventing this in law. If she does not marry before her parents die, she is destitute. And for all their doting on her, they have chosen Sir Richard. She must either accept or starve. To be fair, I believe my uncle and aunt think they are doing their best for her. It is awful, but not an uncommon situation."

"What are you two whispering about?" asked Lucinda crossly.

"Her options are limited," said Mary finally.

I sighed. I could not believe what I was about to say. "Lucinda — Lucy, if I may. I assure you Sir Richard is all too human. I am sure he will be able to offer you a materially comfortable life."

"Well, there is the castle," admitted Lucinda.

As we closed the door behind us, Lucinda now tucked back in bed and asleep, I said to Mary, "I am not happy about this. Richard Stapleford is not a good man."

"Has he unnatural appetites?" asked Mary.

I struggled with this statement for a moment. "I have no idea," I exploded.

"I have heard that you were once his maid and I thought —"

"You are quite correct that Sir Richard makes advances to maids, but I can assure you I repulsed him."

"If he took no for an answer, he is better than most peers of the realm," said Mary.

I gasped.

"I have no high opinion of the male of the species," she said.

"So I understand. This makes your determination to see your cousin married even more striking."

"As we have discussed, she has no other options," said Mary shortly. "I am grateful for your assistance."

I shook my head. "This is a bad night's work," I said.

"Unless you are going to tell me the man is a murderer I cannot see that another man would be a better option."

I opened and then closed my mouth. Given our history there was nothing I could say.

CHAPTER
THIRTEEN

Aspersions at breakfast

"It's all very sad," Bertram said when I told him the tale at breakfast, "but she doesn't sound like the brightest girl. She may well be happy with what Richard offers."

I grimaced.

Bertram blushed red and said quickly, "A lot of ladies have no choice but to lie back and think of England."

"More coffee?" I asked, picking up the coffee pot.

"I mean, well, you know," said Bertram, fingering the edge of his collar. "It's not like many of us marry for love. Is it different with the lower orders, like McLeod?"

The coffee pot hovered over his cup. I did not begin to pour. "McLeod?" I said in a tone that Bertram should have known well.

"He was all up for marrying you for love, until he discovered you were quite bright for a woman. Lucky escape you had there. You got out before people started talking." He took a sip of his own coffee, then said musingly, "I suspect he needs a more amiable, doting sort of bride, though he might not have worked that out yet. Some young thing that will say 'Yes, Rory, no, Rory, oh, you're so wonderful, Rory.' God, imagine the pair of them cooing over breakfast. Be enough to make most men sick."

I barely heard the half of this. The coffee pot wobbled. "Quite bright for a woman?" I asked, my voice rising.

Bertram's eyes flickered from the coffee pot to his cup and to my face. He appeared for the first time to notice the danger he was in and edged closer to the table, attempting to place his lap beneath the wood and out of harm's way. "I mean, gosh, Euphemia, how you do pick one up! I was only trying to allude to the fact that you and Rory . . . After all, you did think yourself in love didn't you?"

I put the coffee pot down. Bertram sighed with relief, though I saw he had noticed I had not yet yielded my grip. "What has Rory to do with this?" I asked, genuinely puzzled.

"Well, I say . . . I mean, it's just . . . you know, the lower classes don't tend to wait until *the day*."

"The day?" I repeated blankly.

"I mean . . . you and old McLeod." Bertram did something extraordinary with his eyebrows. "Doing what nature does best . . . I'm not one to gossip, but if it had gone on much longer someone would have worked it out." He lowered his voice until it was almost inaudible, "That Rory taught you things no lady should know."

His meaning dawned on me. I took several deep breaths. "You are extremely lucky, Bertram Stapleford,"

I said in tones so icy my mother would have been proud, "that I was gently bred, or I would throw this pot at your head."

"Gosh, I mean . . . I just assumed," said Bertram, trying to lever himself away from the table, but his chair arms were well wedged beneath it and there was no escape.

"Bertram, you have made a grievous error in judgement concerning my moral character."

"No idea what came over me," said Bertram desperately.

"But I will have you know that my mother wishes me to go and live at the Palace as soon as her wedding is done."

Bertram positively goggled. "The Palace?"

"Oh, not that one, you idiot! A bishop's residence is called a palace."

"Right. Oh . . . will you go? I don't think Richenda will like that."

"What won't Richenda like?" said the lady in question, sitting down opposite Bertram, who jumped like a scalded cat at her voice, bashing his knees hard under the table. The other breakfast diners, scattered up and down the long table in groups of two or three as is usual at an informal buffet breakfast, turned to stare at Bertram. Fortunately, it was a very long table and we had been speaking softly.[1]

---

[1] Not that discretion would necessarily have occurred to Bertram. One of the few things he has acquired from the upper classes is the notion that he can say what he likes when he likes.

"That the bride has had a dress sent from London and is going to look ravishing," said Bertram, thinking quickly.

Richenda shook her head. "It's her last day of freedom before she's shackled to my brother for life, poor thing. Frankly, I feel I should be giving her a medal." She reached for the toast and took three slices.

Bertram raised an eyebrow. "I thought you would have had breakfast upstairs, seeing how Richard gave you and Hans a suite. I only got a poky little turret room."

"That's a bachelor's lot," said Richenda. "You should get married. And this is baby's breakfast. I've had mine, but he hasn't had his."

"You know it's a boy?" asked Bertram.

Richenda and I exchanged looks. "I have a feeling," she said.

"Don't tell Richard," begged Bertram. "We were going to come to your suite after breakfast and discuss matters." He looked around the room. "Where's Hans?"

"He's playing with Amy," said Richenda.

"Gosh, Richie, is that a German thing? You've got the nursemaid now. I mean, Mother never spent more than half an hour a day with any of us."

"And that worked out well, didn't it?"

"Yes, but the thing is," said Bertram, not listening, "I don't think you should be going around on your own."

"Why ever not?" said Richenda.

Bertram lowered his voice to a whisper, so Richenda had to lean over the table to hear him. Her sleeve inevitably trailed in the jam. "Well, the thing is, Euphemia and I . . . well, the thing is . . ."

"Oh, spit it out, Bertie," said Richenda in exasperation.

Before I could stop him, Bertram said, "We're pretty sure that Richard is going to try and kill you today."

"Today?" echoed Richenda.

"Well . . . maybe not today, but while you're at the castle."

"Did you hear him say this?" asked Richenda. "Don't think for a moment I want to give the cad the benefit of the doubt, but even I see some issues with inviting me up here with a whole host of witnesses, just to bump me off. I would have thought he'd send that weasel of an agent of his down to the estate when Hans was away on business, and got him to do the dirty deed quietly."

"You know, your association with Euphemia is doing you no favours," said Bertram harshly. "That's not the kind of thing a lady should ever think about. I mean, we've all accepted, one way or another, that Euphemia keeps falling over dead bodies, but, honestly, it's not on for *you* to concern yourself with such things."

"I'll have you know I have been very useful," said Richenda crossly. "I found out very important information the last time Euphemia was in jail. And I don't see why you should have all the fun!"

"We were on to the landlady," said Bertram.

"Enough," I hissed before he gave away more than he should. Richenda had no idea that our last escapade had involved the British Secret Service and I wanted to keep it that way. "We had no idea about her, Bertram. Richenda was invaluable."

"Thank you," said Richenda.

"But I do think rather than quibbling about the past we should think about the future and whether the threat is real."

"Why would he?" asked Richenda.

"Because you're with child," said Bertram, and blushed again. "And if nature runs to course, your child will be the first legitimate child born into the family."

"Oh, the Hall," said Richenda, waving her hands about airily. "Forget what I said last night. I admit I wanted to annoy him, but I have no interest in the place. I'm happy on Hans' estate. The Hall has nothing but bad memories for me."

"That's a bit of an about-face," said Bertram.

"Yes, well, what with Amy arriving on the scene, and being pregnant — and Hans, of course — it's all made me think differently about a lot of things. That bloody house has been a curse on our family. Richard thinks the more property and money he can get his hands on, the better life will be, but I've discovered that alongside riding, my greatest pleasure is sitting on the floor in a most unladylike way and playing with my daughter."

"Bravo, Richenda!" I said.

"That's all very well and good," said Bertram, "but that doesn't change the fact that, according to our father's will, the Hall will be yours."

"But I don't want it," said Richenda. "I'll tell Richard he can have it."

"A man's pride," said Bertram.

"He wouldn't," said Richenda, "I mean, I'm sure he wouldn't. Apart from anything it would be too awkward."

"He wouldn't have planned for it," said Bertram. "He didn't know. None of us did. But now he does, he'll have to fudge something."

"Perhaps," I interjected before the argument got more heated, and more to the point, louder, "we should bring Hans in on our discussions and see what he has to say. He is liable to have a less, er, less influenced perspective than any of us."

I expected Richenda to balk at the idea, but instead she clapped her hands. "Excellent," she said. "That's just the thing to stop him fretting about my losing the child, like his first wife always did. He can go all protective." She smiled smugly. "I could enjoy this."

CHAPTER
FOURTEEN

Hans is sensible

Hans took the news that his wife's twin might be intending to kill her surprisingly calmly. We were all seated in the saloon of their suite. Richenda had had tea and cake sent up. I thought, at first, that Hans might not have understood her through the sponge she was currently demolishing.

"I did think about this," he said.

"You did?" I asked, surprised.

Hans reached out and touched his wife's hand. "Not that he would harm Richenda, but that he would certainly be very angry about our child being born first. Do you want to own Stapleford Hall, Richenda?"

Richenda shook her head. She had begun on a custard tart and even she could not speak through that.

"Well, neither do I," said Hans. "You can sign it over to Richard and all will be well. We can make our right to it our wedding gift to the happy couple."

"That's an excellent idea," I said. "Bertram was sure his pride would mean he wouldn't accept it, but he cannot refuse a wedding gift. Especially if Richenda tells his bride what she means to do first."

Hans smiled at me. "Even better," he said. "I imagine that even in Scotland they have lawyers. I shall have the butler telephone for one, and we will draw up the papers today."

Bertram heaved a sign. "All feels a bit of a wash-out now," he said sadly.

"So sorry I am not to be assassinated for your entertainment," said Richenda tartly.

"Oh, I say, sis, you know I didn't mean that! It's just when a man's blood is up . . . it's, well, up."

"Never mind, Bertram," said Hans, "you can guard Richenda until the papers are drawn up. I trust you."

Bertram positively preened at this. "As you want," said Richenda, "I am due in the nursery to have a dolls' tea party with Ellie and Amy. You can play the butler."

Bertram's eyes darted to me. Clearly, this was not what he intended. "Don't look at me," I said. "I need to go and find Mary Hill and see if I can make my peace with her."

Richenda's head came up. "Good luck with that."

"If you will excuse me," said Hans. "I will attend to matters. I will send a footman for you when the papers are ready for your signature."

"You can get them done today?" I asked, surprised. "I pay well and it is not a complicated matter."

And with Hans' singular masterstroke the threat looming over Richenda's head vanished. When we gathered that night to dine, Lucinda glowed with happiness. She and Richenda chatted happily over cocktails. Richard stood a little way back from them with what I assume he took to be a benevolent smile on his face. I knew him well enough to know he was not exactly pleased by Richenda's gift, but, on the other hand, he was not angered either. He had won the day, but more by accident than design and he seemed to feel it.

I could tell Bertram's experience in the nursery had disturbed him greatly. By my count, he was on his fifth cocktail. I had completely failed to track down Mary Hill and had spent the rest of the day in an orgy of reading and silence in my room.[1]

The only interruption had been Enid, who had appeared around lunchtime and been most disturbed to find me in my room.

"Oh, miss, you'll be missing your lunch," was her opening sally.

"I had an excellent breakfast, thank you, Enid, and I have no doubt that Sir Richard will have another very large banquet laid on for us tonight."

"I know how it's not my place to say such things, miss, but it's a lot colder up here than down in your country. You need to eat to keep your strength up."

I looked at her and then pointedly at the roaring fire that I had, in a most unladylike fashion, lit myself. Then it dawned on me. "Enid, could it be that you need to attend to my bedchamber?"

---

[1] Yes, I did say orgy, but please do remember that my excellent father saw I was thoroughly schooled in the Classics. If my mother had known the half of what I learnt from those volumes she would have burnt every book in the house! But neither Greek nor Latin were her forte.

"So sorry, miss. I thought ye'd be out and about, being one o' the younger ones."

"So you left my room to last?"

"Third last," said Enid miserably. "*Please* don't report me to Mrs Lewis, miss. I need this job. There isnae much up here. It was a blessing to us when Sir Richard bought the castle."

"No, Enid, I won't mention this to Mrs Lewis. I appreciate you have a great deal to do. Although, I must say, I found the housekeeper to be a most fair woman."

Enid regarded me quizzically, quite rightly wondering how I had formed an opinion on Mrs Lewis at such short acquaintance. I suppressed an impulse to enlighten her. Heavens, was I actually missing Richenda's inane chatter! However, this feeling was soon to pass, as I discovered that Enid's gratitude at not being exposed to Mrs Lewis was to be shown by her prattling away about the goings-on in the castle from the servants' perspective.

At first, I did my best to tune her out, uttering only a little ladylike "Hmm" now and again to acknowledge I was listening and keeping my eyes firmly on my page. Far too much of her diatribe was about the wonders of Sir Richard and his rescue of the estate. The man she described I barely recognised, but it was undoubtedly the same image that Richard had been projecting to Lucinda, and I still felt uneasy about last night's work.

But then, she said, "And of course the commotion that auld geist is causing downstairs."

"Mr Guscott?" I enquired, thinking she had mispronounced one of the guests' names.

"Och, no, he's a lovely auld gentleman, I've got nae problem with him. No, I mean one o' the castle geists, miss. We've always had a few that walked at nicht. A few wee keeks here and there. The auld piper on the castle wall at dusk, the white lady,[1] the chimney boy that got stuck up the chimney a hundred years or so ago — poor wain always cries when Cook is frying sausages, she says. Seems like it was the poor wee mite's favourite dish. And then there's the Lord and Lady that wander about. Not a couple, but my auld nan said how she thought that after all the time they've began courting as anyone who sees the one tends to see the other too. And then there's yon shepherdess who sometimes wanders into the downstairs necessary, near the kitchen. There used to be a door there before they put the new plumbing in. Apparently, the last Laird lost a butler that way. He was doing his business when she fair breezed through the wall. Said he wouldn't stay in a household where the geists had nae shame!"

She laughed heartily at this last joke.

"You don't find any of these apparitions disturbing?" I asked curiously.

"Och no, miss. Lots of folk in the Highlands have the sight. We're quite used to such things and it's not like they ever do anyone any harm."

"Have you actually seen one?"

"Well, I'm not sure," said Enid, thoughtfully. "There was that nicht Jimmy McCowan got me to try his ma's

---

[1] White ladies are so common that I have resolved never to wear this dangerous colour!

homemade wine. I thought I heard the piper then, but afterwards I reckoned what the noise was, was the bootboy, who'd also got himself a bottle, little blighter, retching up his guts."

"Well, it all sounds most entertaining," I said, turning my page and applying myself once more to my story.

"It is, miss, but the Wailing Nanny is back, and me and some of the other staff are feart if Miss Lucinda hears it she might persuade Sir Richard to sell the castle on, and who knows when we'd find another decent master."

I barely suppressed a snort.

Enid misinterpreted my response. "You might sniff, miss, but the Wailing Nanny is always an omen o' bad fortune."

"Then I suggest you do not repeat the belief in her existence to any other guest."

"The thing is, miss, we were wondering, seeing as how you and Miss Lucinda get on so well, if you might not have a wee word reassuring her."

"Me?" I asked as the realisation dawned that our meeting was no coincidence.

"It's not as if the baby died, like everyone thought. Of course, he didn't exactly have a great life, what with the castle burning down, but they did find him again."

I shook my head in puzzlement. Enid sighed, "I'm not that good at explaining things, miss. My ma says how I always have two tongues once I get going. The Wailing Nanny, miss, was nanny to the last Laird when his son was a wee bairn. Tot must have been only two

or so. Anyway he ups and gets out of the castle —
climbing out one of the windows, they think," I
shuddered, remembering Amy's recent exploits, "and
goes and finds himself a tinker's caravan to hide in. The
tinkers only found him when they had moved on tae
another village."

"Tinkers? Do you mean gypsies?"

"Aye, ye'd call them that, miss. Anyway, the tot not
bein' able to talk properly, it takes them a couple of
days to work out who he is. That's what they said,
anyway. Most folks reckon they kept him a day or two
in the hope that his late Lordship would reward them
well for returning him."

"But he came home safe?"

"Oh, aye, but the Wailing Nanny, she never saw that.
The family put about a story about her packing her
traps in the nicht and leaving, but everyone knew she
had thrown herself off the castle ramparts in shame. It's
said the gardeners had to scrape her up with a shovel!
Now, she wanders at night, crying and looking for the
bairn. It's said she can't rest until she finds him. My
nan said how a nanny that loses a bairn can never get
intae heaven. It's the worst sin ever. She was a nanny
herself. She knew the Wailing Nanny. They'd both
applied for the position, but she didn't get it. My nan,
that is."

"So this is all recent history?"

"Och, no, ancient!" said Enid with the sublime
disregard of a fifteen-year-old, "It must have been thirty
years ago or more!"

"That's not a lot of time for a ghost to build up a reputation," I said.

"Och, I left out the best bit, miss! It was her crying and wailing that alerted the servants when the castle caught fire. Without her waking them they'd have all been burnt in their beds!"

"I see. I take it you weren't working here then?"

"No, but I know the story," said Enid forcefully. "It definitely happened. John Footman swore on his aunt's grave. And she is dead — I asked my nan."

"Well, thank you, Enid. This has all been most enlightening. I am sure that Miss Lucinda will not worry about such things. Indeed, you could say the Wailing Nanny was your guardian angel."

"That's a nice way of looking at it, miss, but she didn't half make a racket last night. Even those used to the castle's ways were disturbed." I thought silently that they might have been indulging without caution in the leftover wine from the banquet. Having seen how things worked behind the green baize door, among the servants, I knew full well that even with the best housekeeper in the world, it was hard to keep the entirety of a large male staff from the after-dinner benefits.

"We just don't want her believing the other stories," said Enid.

"Which ones?"

"The ones of how she scares women into losing their babes."

"What?" I sat bolt upright.

100

"The Laird's wife was carrying when the bairn went missing. My nan says it would just have been the strain, but there's some folks who reckon she makes . . . well, you see what I mean."

"I do indeed," I said. I had no fear for Lucinda, but I could not help wondering if the Wailing Nanny was having some help in walking abroad, and if Richard had not been quite as grateful for Richenda's gift as he had said.

CHAPTER
FIFTEEN

Bertram is jealous

I made my way across the room to Bertram, determined to part him from the cocktail tray. The room was filling up with people. I recognised some of the faces, but I was beginning to realise this set of people were almost entirely from the business or trade world. This made Sir Richard the highest-ranking person there. I could see how this would appeal to his vanity, but I also wondered if he was also shy of displaying his new wife to the aristocratic world that he had always seemed so keen on entering.[1] I was about to quietly enquire from Bertram as to his view on this, when I got close enough to see his complexion. He looked ghastly.

"Are you inebriated?" I demanded under my breath.

Bertram shook his head vigorously and, by the slight stagger he then gave, appeared to immediately regret this forceful action.

"You are!"

"Dash it, Euphemia! You can hardly blame a fellow after what happened. She might have been killed!"

---

[1] Having now attended more than one grand party, and being related to some of the denizens of said world, I could not and still cannot understand his ambition.

I caught a tight hold of his sleeve and as discreetly as I could, but also as forcefully, I led him over to the window, pulling back the drapes slightly under the pretext of pointing out the view. "What has happened?" I demanded. "I have kept to myself all day."

"Can't believe you don't know," said Bertram maddeningly. "I thought he would have made a point of telling you."

"Bertram, I shall stand heavily on your foot if you do not at once reveal what you know."

Bertram swallowed hard. "You don't know Richenda took a tumble down the stairs?"

"Oh, dear God!" I cried. "Is she safe?"

"Hush," said Bertram. "Hans has gone to a lot of trouble to keep this quiet. He got her a doctor of his choosing. Sawbones says it's only a sprain. Though her ankle's swollen up like a giant green balloon. Made me feel quite sick when I saw it."

"The baby?" I said urgently.

"Oh, Amy's fine."

"No, Richenda's!"

"Ah," said Bertram, blushing. "Doctor said there was nothing else to worry about, so I assume that it's still well tethered. Didn't like to pry; female stuff and all that."

"How is Hans?"

"Angry," said Bertram. "She slipped on one of Amy's toys and he blames the new nursery nurse. Though we both know what Amy's like. Any room she's in looks like an earthquake has hit it within a quarter of an hour of her starting to play."

I nodded. Amy's untidiness was legendary. She remained the only person to have ever brought Hans' stoic butler, Stone, to his knees — with the help of her marbles.

"Where was Ellie?"

"I got the impression," said Bertram, colouring even more deeply, "from Richenda that she was attending to a natural function. Richenda thought that Ellie had been away some time, and she was feeling the need to rest, so she opened the door and took a few steps along the corridor to find the girl."

"Will she ever learn to pull the bell and not see to things herself?" I demanded in despair. I was about to develop my theme on how Richenda needed to become more genteel, when Bertram interrupted with a comment that took my breath away.

"'Course, it wasn't the poor girl's fault. It was Richard who put it there."

I regarded him blankly.

"Think about it, Euphemia! She went out the door. The toy was outside the nursery. Amy has never been allowed to play by the stairs."

"You know Amy's propensity for getting into places where she should not —" I began. Bertram cut me short.

"She's been under someone's eye every moment she's been here. Hans has been most insistent. Bit of a surprise, really. I mean, he's about to get one of his own, you might think he wouldn't . . ."

"Hans is not like that," I said shortly. "He adopted Amy and he loves her as if she is her own."

"Yes, I am aware that, according to you, he's a perfect paragon," said Bertram sharply. "Unlike my own brother, who, despite getting the wretched homestead, is still intent on offing his twin. Can't stand to be beaten at anything. Always been the same. You know, I used to choose the weakest conkers on purpose. It tended to get painful if I ever won."

"I suppose he might have feared that a document drawn up under Scottish law might not be strong enough to hold up in England," I said thoughtfully, "but to attempt to kill his sister — and at his own wedding!"

"Exactly," said Bertram. "Now, if you will excuse me, I have an appointment with the contents of a cocktail shaker. Try and stay with the herd, Euphemia, I don't want to see Richard getting cocky and trying to take you out as an encore. You know you've always been a thorn in his side." And with that extraordinary statement he set off across the room, weaving easily between the guests. It was only when he tried to walk straight that his state became most apparent.

"I take it he has told you everything," said Hans' voice at my elbow.

I spun around. "It is true? Are they both safe? Richenda and her baby?"

Hans' rather grim expression broke into a smile. "The doctor said he had never met a tougher lady. He has no fears. Though he did suggest Richenda might cut down on her intake of cake."

"And he still lives?" I asked, with a shaky smile.

"I pointed out that Richenda has a constitution that needs cake and all was well. I think he quickly realised his error. The look she gave him could have felled an army."

"I know you are making light of the situation to put me at my ease, but do you agree with Bertram's theory?"

Hans shook his head. "I cannot believe it. I think it much more likely that our new nursery maid is slipshod at her work. I blame myself for engaging her on so little knowledge."

"Perhaps no one is to blame," I said, putting a hand lightly on his arm. "Sometimes accidents simply happen."

"Perhaps," said Hans, "but I appear to have married into a family that has more issues than one would find in an old-fashioned gothic novel."

I smiled at him. "And yet I am sure you regret nothing."

Hans smiled back at me. "Almost nothing," he said. "Why don't we defy convention and sit together at dinner?"

"And upset Richard's careful table arrangement?"

Hans gave a flicker of a wink. "I feel it is the least I can do."

I laughed and agreed, which I was soon to regret, for our seating arrangement drew some attention. Even Bertram looked shocked. No one commented aloud, but I realised that perhaps accompanying my handsome, charming employer into dinner while his wife was indisposed and pregnant was not my wisest decision. I decided that there was nothing to do but brazen it out. Accordingly, I regaled Hans with Enid's colourful stories, causing him not inconsiderable amusement. Bertram's looks became darker and darker.

Once dinner was over, the ladies withdrew to take tea, but in a very short period of time some of the gentleman joined us. The wedding was to be tomorrow and there was too much to discuss for the party to stay separate. Bertram, who now seemed remarkably sober, came over to me, clutching his teacup so tightly his knuckles showed white.

"Where is Hans?" he demanded.

"Perhaps he has gone up to see Richenda?" I suggested. "Or is playing billiards?"

"You don't know?"

"No."

Bertram uttered what can only be described as a snort. "Well, we need to find him. Rory has something to tell us."

CHAPTER
SIXTEEN

A mathematician sees a ghost

"Do we need Hans?" I asked. "You know how they rub each other up the wrong way."

"I don't need Hans," said Bertram.

"Do you have something in your eye? You appear to be squinting."

"That, Euphemia, is my disapproving look," said Bertram. "I suppose we had better do without him. Meet you by the servants' stairs nearest the kitchen in ten minutes."

"Can we not meet him in your room? I would rather not be caught skulking around the backstairs."

"Oh no," said Bertram, "you had much better be caught in my chambers."

"But Rory would be there."

Bertram shook his head slowly from side to side. He appeared to have learned his lesson from earlier about waggling it too fast. "Oh, Euphemia, you know so little about the ways of the world."

"That's quite a change from what you said earlier," I replied tartly.

"It is not my fault that your behaviour often leads others to unfortunate conclusions," said Bertram.

Before I could muster a reply he had slunk off. I would have to save my ripostes until later. I lingered by the tea tray in the hope that my upcoming exit would not be linked with Bertram's.

"I need to thank you for speaking to Lucy last night. She is now much more settled in her mind."

I turned to find Mary Hill standing before me, a glass of what looked remarkably like port in her hand.

"As I said at the time, I am unconvinced it remains a good night's work."

"And, as I said, Lucy's options are limited." Although she had approached me with words of thanks, I detected in Miss Hill's eyes and general manner her continued dislike of me.

"Is there anything else I can help you with?" I asked.

"You need to understand that, intellectually, Lucy is not well-endowed. Neither is she a girl of spirit."

"Ah, I see. You are not happy about the situation either," I said.

"You mistake me, Miss St John. I make no excuses for persuading her into the marriage. She is unlike us. She does not have strength of character."

"Why, Miss Hill, is this a compliment?" I smiled.

"One should never confuse character with goodness or even with intelligence," retorted Mary.

"But I thought you excelled at mathematics?"

"I do," said Mary. Then she sighed. "It was not my intention to quarrel with you. It is only that I have been hearing the strangest stories about the castle, and am now somewhat concerned . . ."

"If you are referring to the fire," I answered, "it happened long before Sir Richard took ownership. I believe it has been fully and safely restored."

"That is something of a relief."

"Which part?" I asked, but Mary ignored my question.

"I have also learned that the locals believe in ghosts and are certain this place is haunted. I would not like Lucy to learn of this. It will distress her."

"The castle being one of her main inducements to marry Sir Richard," I suggested.

Mary had the grace to blush. "I do not believe in such things, but I would rather Lucy was not frightened by such tales."

"From my experience of visiting the Highlands, and the Scottish in general," I said, mentally excluding a certain butler from my list, "the local people are most keen on the telling of ghost stories. A great many of them claim to have 'the sight' and to be in general communion with the dead. But the weather is so very bad up here, and they have neither of the resources of good shopping nor theatre to entertain them: I fear it is a necessary pastime. While there are many people clustered around the castle, Scotland is in general, I believe, a sparsely populated land. I have had occasion to walk through some of the wilder, wooded parts of the country, and it is not difficult to understand where the local belief in superstitions may spring from."

"But you do not believe in such nonsense?" demanded Mary.

I hesitated. "I have seen enough of life and death to make me perhaps more receptive to such ideas than I once was, but I am in no way a believer."

"That is no answer at all," said Mary, giving me a look that reminded me her mathematical world was one of absolutes.

"I am sorry. I do not have a better one."

"I suppose I am left with no option but to tell you what I saw," said Mary. "Please, do not give sway to groundless superstition. Lucinda is too nervous about everything for me to confide in her and Sir Richard is obviously much engaged with his guests. It seems I have no option but to rely on your opinion for guidance."

I repressed the urge to apologise again.

Mary sighed. "Although it is winter and the night comes quickly this far north, I have also found that the moonlight appears more effective than in England. I have come to the conclusion that this is something to do with the general darkness of the castle and its environs and our eyes adjusting to the dark, coupled with the lack of streetlamps. This gives the illusion of many things outside being outlined in silver and surprisingly visible."

I probed through her sentences, trying to make sense of them. "Do you mean you have seen a ghost?" I asked, surprised.

"I do not believe in such things," said Mary hotly. I raised an eyebrow and, giving another large sigh, she continued. "The first night I was here I drew my curtains open after dark to inspect the stars. I have a minor interest in astronomy, and, as I have indicated, there are scientific reasons why the heavens are clearer up here . . ."

"But you saw something else?"

"I would have thought nothing of it, but I saw the same thing again last night and I have a growing suspicion I will see the same tonight."

This time I suppressed an urge to shake her. "And that was?"

"A silver figure walking towards the area of the castle that is yet to be refurbished since the fire. I believe it was a stable block."

"Could it not have been a servant?"

"Why would someone be heading towards a deserted part of the castle late at night? I am afraid some villainy is afoot. I thought, considering your propensity to see murderers everywhere, that you would be more concerned. I have no idea to whom I should report my sightings."

"And you do not want to be thought foolish?" I asked.

"I do not wish to raise unnecessary alarums on the eve of Lucinda's wedding, but neither do I wish to overlook something I may later have cause to regret."

"So you want me to look into it?" I asked.

"I want you to tell me who to inform!" she said. "I have little reason to trust your detective abilities."

I bit my lip. I could understand her sentiment, but unfortunately, I was prevented from explaining that, in the end, I had indeed caught the murderer who had landed us all in jail. The person in question had taken their own life and the matter, for the sake of their family, was closed. "I met a footman called Rupert. I think he has duty on our floor. He might be the one to question. He worked at the castle before the fire. I believe Sir Richard's Land Agent might also be here, but he does not have an approachable personality.[1] I am afraid I have not yet encountered the butler. He would be the person to deal with this kind of situation. But there are so many of us guests and, it appears, at least twice as many staff!"

Mary looked a little startled. "More than one servant per person?"

I gave her a pitying look. It never failed to surprise me that no matter how intelligent the speaker they generally failed to appreciate how very many people were needed to keep any great houses, or even middle-sized houses, running. "Swans," I muttered under my breath. Among the privileged, it all glided along smoothly, while below stairs the servants toiled and sweated. Despite this, my sojourn of working below stairs had yielded my closest friends and some of the people I rate most highly. Despite her support of the Suffragettes, the women's group intended to encompass all classes, Mary clearly remained unaware of the lot of the lower classes.

"Or, if you prefer, you could go straight to the housekeeper, Mrs Lewis," I added. "She previously worked at Stapleford Hall and is a very straight forward and sensible woman, not in the least given to gossip."

---

[1] Ha!

"Yes, I suppose that sounds best. How would I go about it?"

"If you want to do such a thing quietly, I would ask the maid who has been allocated to you to mention to Mrs Lewis that you wished to speak to her. She would respond as soon as she was able, I am sure."

"Very well, that is what I will do."

"I confess I do not understand your concern, Mary — Miss Hill, I mean. It is probably only a wandering tramp seeking refuge from the cold."

"Yes, no doubt," said Mary. "But I will feel happier when someone investigates."

"If you will excuse me, I have arranged to meet up with an acquaintance this evening," I said.

"Thank you for your time, Miss St John," she said, and turned away. I walked slowly to the door and once it closed behind me, bolted down the hall. I was late to meet Bertram.

CHAPTER
SEVENTEEN

Rory is suspicious

I found both Bertram and Rory waiting for me by the servants' stairs. Rory was standing impassively, hands behind his back, while he examined the vaulted ceiling. Bertram was pacing back and forth, fob watch in his hand. He turned at the sound of my footsteps. "Where have you been?" he hissed in a loud whisper. Then he grabbed my arm and pulled me through the baize door into the servants' passage. Rory followed, but I thought I heard him sigh.

We stood on a little landing, the bare stone steps curling up and down what appeared to be a servants' turret. "Where have you been?" repeated Bertram.

I leaned over the iron rail and peered down the staircase. No electricity or even gas lamps lit this stairway. What little light we had came from Rory keeping his foot half in the doorway, allowing some light from the castle hallway to creep in. I sneezed. The stone felt gritty under my shoe.

"Same as ever," said Rory. "All show on the front and behind the scenes a somewhat more dire situation."

"It's too dark," I said. "We cannot know if we are being overheard."

"Does it matter?" asked Rory.

"As Bertram has dragged us into this dingy . . ." I sneezed again, "and extremely dusty hole, I assume he does not want to be overheard."

"And a slightly ajar servant's door and loud whispering will naturally bar all notice," said Rory wryly.

"Could we not simply find one of the lesser-used rooms?" I asked. "The place seems big enough." I sneezed again. "My eyes are starting to water."

"Oh, lass, you've become weak and pallid among the fine folk," mocked Rory.

Bertram fairly bounced on the balls of his feet with frustration. Rory took pity on him. "This way," he said, and he led us, always staying three paces ahead like a good footman, back through the baize door and towards the back of the castle.

"He can't do this," whispered Bertram to me. "He's a valet. He will arouse suspicion."

"As you well know, he is actually a butler by trade and, I suspect, by temperament. He could look down his nose at a Duchess, if she used the wrong fork, and get away with it. I'm betting that no one will interrupt our passage."

"Unless we come across someone we all know," muttered Bertram darkly.

Rory had us quickly at a small saloon, decorated startlingly in yellow and green tartan. No one was in there for the simple reason that it was as cold as an icehouse. There was no fire, so I helped Rory start one. Bertram looked on in awe, as if we were conjuring the flames with mystical powers. Within a very short time, we had a roaring blaze. Then the three of us drew chairs around the hearth and settled down to talk.

"This is rather nice, isn't it?" I said, thinking aloud. "Companionship by the fireside and not a murder in sight."

Rory threw me a strange look. Bertram said, "Do not tempt fate, Euphemia. It is only by the grace of God that Richenda was not more badly hurt."

"Bertram, have you ever considered that perhaps we look too hard for mysteries? Could this not only be an unfortunate accident?"

Bertram opened and closed his mouth several times, but no sound emerged.

"I, for one, do not believe it to be an accident," interrupted Rory, "and that is the reason I wished to speak with you. I am not comfortable about that Susie Ellis."

Bertram found his voice. "McLeod, we should call her Ellie like Amy does, to avoid confusion."

Rory shrugged. "If you wish. *Ellie* appears to me to be most distracted. On more than one occasion I have found her some distance from the nursery suite, in areas of the castle I believe she had no cause to be."

"Was she lost?" I asked.

"That was, indeed, what she would have had me believe," said Rory.

"But you don't?" said Bertram.

"I cannot put my finger upon it precisely," said Rory, "but she doesnae feel right. I have worked with many servants now and there is something that's not quite right. Not in the same way as I knew from the first that there was something wrong with Euphemia."

"I am sitting right here," I protested. "Besides, there is nothing wrong with me."

Rory looked at Bertram. "I knew she was hiding secrets from us all."

I paled slightly. It was true: Rory had been the only one to doubt my persona as a bona fide servant, from almost the moment he met me. I knew his judgement to be acute when his feelings were not too deeply involved.

"Did you ever get her to tell you what they were?" asked Bertram curiously.

"I am still here," I said, pronouncing each word with considerable weight.

"No," said Rory. "I did not."

"Did you know her mother is about to marry a bishop?"

Rory raised an eyebrow. "Interesting."

"So are you suggesting Ellie is hiding something?" I asked, desperate to draw the attention away from myself. Their tone had been jocular and I knew in their own way they only meant to tease, but I was not ready to reveal to either of them my true ancestry. Although I feared if my mother got her way they would, all too soon, know all my secrets.

Rory shrugged. "I don't know that I can say, more than she feels wrong."

"Have you ever found her outside the castle?" I asked, a thought striking me.

Rory shook his head. "No. She might be able to convince me to give her the benefit of the doubt if she has lost her way in the corridors, but were I to come across her in the castle grounds I would have to draw Mr Muller's attention to it."

"And you have reason to go back and forth to see to the automobile?" I asked.

"It's not a horse, Euphemia," said Bertram. "It doesn't need feeding. Besides, Rory is acting as my valet."

"I do go out from time to time," interrupted Rory. "In this weather it is not a bad idea to turn the engine over every now and then, and tomorrow — if you can spare me, Bertram — I thought I might have a look at the spark plugs. The trip up here being her first run, I'd like to take a proper keek under the bonnet, make sure it's all fine. The last thing I want is to break down when we are on our way home," he finished, leaving us all with the thought of how little we would like to be stranded at the castle.

"But it's the wedding!" protested Bertram.

"Aye, I ken," said Rory, suddenly going very Scotch. "I wasnae aware I was invited."

"Well, you're not, but . . ."

"I'll make sure you're all kitted out and then I thought I'd away to the garage. One of the kitchen maids has said how she'll bring me out sandwiches."

I raised an eyebrow at this and Bertram, catching my eye, coughed loudly, "A good plan, McLeod. The house will be in chaos."

"Does that mean we need extra eyes on Richenda?" I asked.

"I think Richard will be too caught up with his new bride to worry about Richenda tomorrow," said Bertram.

"And tomorrow night," added Rory.

"Quite," said Bertram shortly, "I think if Richenda takes reasonable precautions she will be perfectly safe. As Lucinda has decided she wants to embrace the Scottish tradition of walking to the local church, Richenda won't even be attending. She'll wait at the castle for the congregation to return for the wedding breakfast."

"We are meant to walk down to the village church?" I asked. "I mean, that is a sweet custom, but it's not as if the Staplefords are known here."

"Hardly the Laird, you mean?" said Rory. "Maybe not the historical Laird, but they've brought a guy lot of employment to the area. Stapleford's even convinced the Laird's son, who lives in a big house in the village to come. He wanted his father to come too, from what I've heard, but the old man must be pushing ninety. Still, you're right in thinking *that* is the local family here. Stapleford is merely the banker."

"The old family did not move away after the fire?" I asked.

"From what I have learnt . . ." said Rory.

"I do not pay you to gossip with the servants," said Bertram hotly. I suspected he was beginning to feel left out.

"I thought, seeing as this is Sir Richard's house, it was worth seeing the lay of the land," said Rory softly.

Bertram huffed. "I suppose you are right."

"As I was saying, the old Laird and his family moved into the largest house in the village. The servants believe he speculated on the stock market in the hopes of raising the funds to rebuild the castle, but did not have much luck."

"Is he bankrupt?" I asked. "Did he have dealings with Richard's bank?"

"That is not impossible," said Bertram. "That may be how Richard heard about the castle in the first place. But it would have to have been the son, not the old man."

"Yes," said Rory. "It seems the family tried for the better part of two generations to hold on to the land, but Stapleford's generous offer came at the right time. I would not be surprised if Stapleford sold it as being best for the local people too. He learnt a lot from his dealings at his Highland lodge."

I shivered, remembering my unfortunate experiences there.[1]

"I think," said Bertram suddenly, "that Euphemia should stay with Richenda."

"And miss the wedding?" said Rory. "Oooh, man, ye have a nerve to ask that of a lassie."

"I am not a man," said Bertram. I saw Rory suppress a smile. "I am a gentleman!"

---

[1] Although to be fair, Rory's had been far more deadly and here he was speaking about it all quite calmly.

Before the serious bickering could commence, I interrupted, "I would much rather not have to gaze on Richard's face as he takes his bride to be his wife. There seems no harm in Lucinda and I feel rather sorry for her."

"Euphemia," said Rory warningly, "I hope you're not going to interfere."

"It might surprise you to know that only last night I was asked to help persuade the young woman to go ahead with the wedding — and I did."

"Euphemia!" gasped Bertram.

"She has few options," I said defensively, "and we have seen Richard show her nothing but kindness."

"If you are about to say you think he has changed —" began Bertram.

"No, of course not. I believe him to remain the dangerous, greedy, self-centred murderer we all secretly think him to be — but I suspect all of us would be in much greater danger if he felt himself crossed."

"I don't know if I should be impressed by your practicality," said Rory, "or depressed by your flexible morality. Ye were always such a defender of the weak and innocent."

I blushed furiously, "I hope I still am, but I am now wise enough to know that one must work within the confines of society — especially if one is a female — and . . . and . . . and I don't think she's actually in danger from him, do you?" I finished weakly.

"Frankly, I have no idea," said Bertram.

"Oh, don't look at me as if I have disappointed you," I snapped back. "I will stay back with Richenda.

If you feel you have a strong objection to the marriage, Bertram, you can jolly well speak up at the ceremony!"

CHAPTER
EIGHTEEN

Richenda denied cake

The next morning found me sitting with a grumpy Richenda in her suite, drinking coffee and eating savoury pastries. We were devoid even of Amy's friendly chatter, as at the last minute Lucinda had asked her to be a flower girl. "Are you certain she did not mention me when she proposed the walk to the church?" asked Richenda, for the hundredth time.

"As I keep telling you, I knew nothing about it until Bertram told me last night."

"It is solely to ensure I do not attend," moaned Richenda.

"I do not think Lucinda has a malicious nature."

"No, more likely it is my brother," said Richenda, her face contorting in a fearsome scowl. "You do not know how lucky you are not to have a twin, Euphemia. He has brought me nothing but trouble."

As I considered this to be perfectly true, there was nothing I could say. I offered Richenda a plate of sweet pastries that appeared to have escaped her attention. She waved them away brusquely. "Can't abide the sight of 'em," she said.

"But there are custard-filled horns here. Your favourite."

Richenda's colour suddenly became tinged with an unflattering shade of green. "Oh, Euphemia," she wailed. "It is terrible. I cannot abide sweet things. They make me as sick as a dog!"

"Good heavens!" I was amazed. Cake had always been the way to improve Richenda's temper. If I was to be denied this weapon, I was unsure how we would all survive the mood swings of her advancing pregnancy.

"I know," said Richenda. "I thought I was seriously ill; that something terrible had happened during my fall."

My mind boggled trying to fit this together.

"But the doctor said it is quite normal for ladies in delicate situations to take some foods into aversion during the latter stages of their confinements. But why, why did it have to be cake?"

I felt Richenda's pain or, more to the point, I anticipated our pain to come. "Did Lucinda find Amy a dress?" I asked, hoping that talk of her daughter would distract her.

Richenda picked up a pastry filled with tomato and some green herb. "Very exotic," she murmured.

"The dress?"

"No, silly, this thing," she said, waving the foodstuff at me. "The dress was rather simple for my taste, but Amy thought she looked like a fairy princess. Apparently Richard has hired a seamstress for Lucinda, so she can have anything she wants made up at any time."

"Hans hired one too," I pointed out.

"Hmm — but ours has no style or taste."

I cast around desperately to change the conversation again. Richenda's taste, particularly her green and orange designs, is not to most other people's tastes. Fortunately, or unfortunately, depending on how you look at it, she is married to a gentleman of impeccable taste and sartorial elegance. "McLeod told me he has met Ellie in unlikely places," I said.

Richenda shrugged. "She might consider him a good prospect. You met her brother. She is doubtless wishful to change her situation. McLeod has a good career ahead of him. She could do worse." She eyed me keenly. "Unless you wish me to dismiss her?"

"I have no further interest in Rory McLeod," I said, although in my heart I was unsure if this was true.

"Good," said Richenda. "It's all very well him working for Bertram, but Hans could not possibly have him in our household. Despite the obligation we both owe him, Hans finds him a difficult man to tolerate. And I would hate to lose you."

"I think being forced to live at Bertram's ever-crumbling estate in the marshy fens would put most women off marrying Rory!" I said with a snort.

"I keep forgetting you spent some time there," said Richenda. "Was it very bad?"

"One of the least eventful days was the morning when the kitchen floor gave way."

"Oh dear, Bertram is so impulsive. He should never have sunk all his money into that terrible place."

My eyes pricked up as I remembered something Rory had implied and then, annoyingly, refused to elaborate on. "All?" I asked. "I thought Bertram was well-situated."

"Hans tells me it is not proper to talk about money, but I do believe Bertram is now struggling for funds. He was meant to be helping Hans meet business people here, but Richard's cronies are not as familiar to him as he had hoped. I would not be surprised if it was Hans who ended up helping Bertram with his investments."

It flashed into my mind that this meant Bertram might have had a reason to want Richenda to lose her child. As she had remarked, he was a man of impulse and passion. I would not put it past him, when he fell in love, to marry the girl within the month. In fact, this had almost happened, but the unfortunate lady had brought an end to his courtship with her sudden demise.

I shook myself. How could I think such a terrible thing of Bertram? Of all the Staplefords he was by far the best. It was this castle: despite the renovations and the bright fires that blazed in all the public and guest rooms, the place felt dark and gloomy to me. I could not rid myself of the feeling that something terrible would soon occur.

I realised Richenda was still talking. "A stable block! I ask you. She doesn't even ride. And Richard is only interested in automobiles. The man is completely besotted. Either that or he thinks that without gifts there is no way she will consent to give him an heir."

"Richenda!" I cried, shocked.

"Oh, don't look at me like that," said Richenda, her eyes alarmingly filling with tears. "I used to do everything he asked of me, but my twin, he never . . . He never . . . I can only think he is most unnatural . . ." Her speech was interrupted by sobs. "He never treated me as he should. He never did anything for me. He never showed me any brotherly affection and, yet, for this girl he has known but five minutes he would move the earth. How can he be so uncaring about his own twin?" she finished on a wail.

It took some time and several fresh pastries to calm her. The mood swings of a lady in an interesting situation are, as Rory once put it, "fearsome times." I managed to walk the tricky line between reminding her of her good fortune in securing such an excellent husband and sounding envious. In the distance I heard the sound of bells. "Listen," I said. "They must be married. Bertram did not object!"

"Did you think he might?"

"At breakfast either his conscience or the kippers were troubling him. I was not sure which."

Richenda gave a little hiccupping laugh. Then she became serious. "Do you think any of us should have warned her what Richard is truly like?"

"We would have done nothing but harm," I said. "I spent a lot of time thinking about this and I do not see how we could have proved his true character to her. He has avoided arrest, and I believe he is responsible for more than one atrocity, but there is no proof."

"He's damnably cunning. I will give him that."

"And, besides, could it not be possible that Lucinda is his Achilles heel? I mean — he does actually love her?"

128

"Euphemia, this habit of trying to see the good in everyone will only get you into difficulties. You must drop it," said Richenda. She cocked her head to one side. "You were right, I hear bells too. I must look a fright. Ring for my maid, Euphemia. I need to bathe and dress. If they are walking back I should have time."

I did so. Then I retired to my room to tidy my hair and wash my face. The wedding breakfast would be served when the guests returned. I could, of course, avoid it by simply staying in my room. But, like a moth drawn to a flame, I felt impelled to attend.

I was making my way downstairs and trying to decide where I could best, and most unobtrusively, await the wedding party. The last thing I wanted to do was make an entrance. I hoped to mix in with the arrivals quite unobserved. What Richenda might do, I could not say, but I thought it better to make my own way. I had almost gained the large hall, which ran from the main doors to the Great Hall and was lined with many smaller saloons, when, as I turned the last corner of the turret stair, I practically collided with Mrs Lewis.

"Oh, Miss St John," she cried stepping back.

I found I sprung back up three steps with the alacrity of a startled cat. This was most embarrassing. I had no knowledge of the cause of Mrs Lewis' facial disfigurement, but I had always done my best to ignore it. However, in the gloomy, dark stairway of an eerie castle, her appearance had made my heart feel as if it had detached itself and leapt into my mouth.

I took a deep breath. "I am so sorry, Mrs Lewis. It was quite my fault. I had been keeping Mrs Muller company and I was looking for a way to quietly join the wedding party upon their return."

"So you heard the bells too?" asked Mrs Lewis. "A difficult time." The last words were spoken almost to herself. Her whole demeanour was most unlike the efficient woman I had previously known.

"Is something troubling you, Mrs Lewis?" I asked. "Can I be of any help?"

This outrageous suggestion from a guest quite snapped her out of her revelry.

"Oh dear me, no." I thought I saw a slight glint in her eye when she continued, "I am afraid I could not imagine you taking on any kind of position at the castle. Although they will need a new housekeeper."

"You are leaving?" I asked, surprised.

"It was only ever intended my being here for setting up the castle. Obviously I know it well." I must have looked blank as she continued, "You know I used to work here for the previous Laird, don't you?"

"It may have been mentioned," I murmured, unsure.

"Anyway, this will not be the primary home for Sir Richard and Lady Stapleford. It is far too out of the way, and Sir Richard has decided he wants me to oversee all his staff, but particularly at the Stapleford Estate, where he intends to mostly reside. I may also be taken to the family's London home when the House is sitting. Parliament," she added.

"Indeed," I said. "It sounds as if your career is flourishing, Mrs Lewis. Having had the privilege of working under you, I know it is well deserved. I wish you all the best. And you are quite right, I do not intend to ever enter the Staplefords' service again."

"If you will forgive me saying so, Miss St John, you should not be in service at all."

I was spared replying to this unusually direct comment from the housekeeper by the sound of voices and footsteps approaching. Mrs Lewis cast a glance over my shoulder and paled. "If you will excuse me," she said, and actually brushed past me in her rush to get away.

I looked round at once to see if I could pick out who she was so desperate to avoid. Richard, his bride on his arm, strode through the hall. Following just behind were two men in kilts. There was a resemblance in their features, but while one was a young man with fiery hair, the other was a gentleman bent and grey. He walked with the aid of a cane and the arm of the younger man, who I assumed to be his son.

Richard and Lucinda swept by me without acknowledgement. Lucinda was beaming up at her new husband, a picture of radiance, but Richard deliberately snubbed me, so perhaps it was not surprising that the young man called out to me, "You there! Where can my father get a chair?"

A little nonplussed at his attitude, I said as politely as I could, "I am afraid I do not know, sir. I am not aware which rooms are to be opened up."

"Good grief, girl. Do you not know who we are? This is the Laird, Fraser Kennedy, the previous owner of this castle, and I am his son, Dougal. Move, you dunderheid!

CHAPTER
NINETEEN

Fate accompli (pun intended)

I drew myself up to my full height, which is admittedly not great, and said with icy politeness, "Allow me to ring for a footman."

Dougal Kennedy frowned fiercely.[1] It was at this point Bertram trundled around the corner. I say trundled, for it seemed all too likely that he had provided himself with a hip flask for the ceremony and had been partaking of it throughout. "What's happening, Euphemia?" he asked, or at least I presumed that was what he asked. It sounded rather like "Wafftshappenin, Iffena?" Then he took in Fraser Kennedy's tottering steps. "Oh dear. Oh dear me," he said, scuttling to the Laird's side. "Looks like you could do with a bit of a hand — a wee bit of a hand. That's what you chaps say, isn't it? Did I tell you my valet is Scotch? Good man. Good worker. Sort of butler-cum-valet." By this point he had reached the

---

[1] I know I should not take a person in aversion due to physical features, but I confess I have never been a fan of bushy ginger eyebrows. Unless the gentleman has an excellent valet, they look, for all the world as if a dead squirrel has been plastered across the gentleman's forehead. Dougal Kennedy clearly had no such servant in his employ.

other side of the Laird, relieved him of his cane and taken his other arm. "Your people can turn their hands to anything, can't they?" continued Bertram, blithely unaware of how insulting he was being. "Comes of living in such a rough country, what? Can't exactly ring up Fortnum's when you need a new jar of marmalade, hmm?"

I tried to catch his eye, but he had started to walk off at quite a pace, so that to keep up with him Dougal was obliged to raise his father's other arm higher. By the time they had reached the end of the hall, both of the Laird's feet were off the ground, and Dougal was red in the face and puffing. I hurried after them; all thoughts of entering unobtrusively lost in my concern that alcohol was masking Bertram's heart problems, and that at any minute he might collapse.

But my worries were in vain. By the time I caught them up, Bertram had deposited the old Laird in his seat at the wedding breakfast table and was toddling off to find his own position. He lurched up to me and offered his arm. "Help you to your seat, milady?" he slurred.

"I imagine I am somewhere at the back," I said drily.

"Not at all," said Bertram, escorting me much further up the table than I had expected. "I am on your right and Hans is on your left. Try not to flirt with him too much. Women in delicate positions, I am told, can feel quite vulnerable. Not that I would have used vulnerable as a word to describe Richenda," he said, pulling out my seat, "She's vulnerable in the way a dreadnought is."

"How much was there in your flask?" I asked quietly. "And how much is left?"

"Have a heart, Euphemia!" said Bertram. "I had to get through the ceremony somehow. Took all the willpower I had not to object when the Minister asked if anyone knew any reason they should not be married. Only reason I didn't was all I could think of to say was, 'because the man's a bloody cad', and it didn't seem right to swear in church." At this point he hiccupped loudly. Hans and Richenda appeared through the crowd to take their seats.

"Goodness, Bertram," said Richenda, "I do believe you're squiffy."

"Not every day one sees a lovely young girl married off to a monster," said Bertram, darkly.

"Hush," I said. "Whatever you feel, it is too late now. They are married in the eyes of God, for better or for worse."

Bertram rolled an eye. "You believe all that rot, don't you?"

"What do you mean?" I asked, shocked.

"In marriage. Ever seen a happy marriage, Euphemia? 'Cause I can tell you my parents were as about as happy as pigs living next to an abattoir."

"Hans and I are perfectly happy," said Richenda crushingly. "Now do be quiet, Bertram, before someone hears you."

"Ah, yes, but *you're* different," said Bertram. "It's not as if you married for . . ." at this point I trod heavily on his foot. He gave an indignant squeak and looked at me with sorrowful eyes. Meanwhile, Hans got a

134

servant's attention and ordered some strong black coffee. When it arrived he handed it to Bertram.

"Drink this before you make a complete fool of yourself," he said softly and with a surprising amount of menace in his voice.

Bertram, looking all too much like a wounded spaniel, muttered apologies and sipped his hot beverage while the rest of the guests took their seats around us. Unbelievably a gong sounded and a man dressed in black livery, presumably the butler, announced, "Please be upstanding for Sir Richard and the new Lady Stapleford."

I was not entirely sure that this was the correct address. Lucinda only had a title due to her husband, so surely she was Lady Richard? Sometimes[1] I missed my mother.

Despite my qualms, everyone else, ladies included, scraped back their chairs and stood. Richenda was the only one who stayed seated. There was an outbreak of cheering from the men as Richard and Lucinda entered. Lucinda's eyes shone like stars. And why not: today she was the Princess of the Castle, and if she had not yet realised the frog-like tendencies of her Prince, who was I to spoil her day? The poor woman would be spending the rest of her life with Richard.

"And bearing his children," whispered Richenda, as if reading my thoughts. I could not repress a shudder. Richard had once tried to kiss me and the memory of his whiskers on my lips still gave me nightmares.

---

[1] Though rarely.

After this came the feast — the many expected courses and many, many glasses of wine. However, Lucinda, or Mrs Lewis, had opted to bring scores of servants so we could all be served as much or as little as we required. The bride and groom were served first, but there were so many guests that they did not bother waiting until everyone was served. Course after course appeared, and while it would be considered rude to turn away the main dish of a course, one could fortunately, as a lady, restrict one's intake without causing comment. Hans, who retains a trim figure, was moderate in his intake from the start. Bertram started by apparently trying to eat for Scotland, but quickly began to flag. Later, he told me that whole banquet struck him as a never-ending nightmare of black arms proffering him more and more food until he feared he might burst. Richenda kept up a snide commentary to Hans about the excess of food until he told her bluntly to desist. Then she lapsed into a sullen silence.

The meal continued with Bertram growing more and more quiet as he struggled to keep his digestion under control. Ever polite, Hans engaged me in small talk. However, as the majority of subjects that interested us both were not ones we wished to share with other guests, our range of topics was somewhat limited. Eventually, we fell back to chatting about the Mullers' estate and Hans' plans for it. I was happy to engage with this, including Hans' future plans for expansion and his desire to become better acquainted with his neighbours. We had almost reached the stage where the bride's father was expected to stand and deliver his speech when I noticed the furious looks Richenda was sending me. I sighed. Offending Richenda had become tiresomely easy since the incipience of her pregnancy.

The speeches were all that was to be expected and none of which I believed for a moment. Richard, as a politician, has become an accomplished speaker, but I closed my ears to him. Finally, Lucinda rose and the ladies left to tidy themselves before the dancing that evening. I retreated quickly to my room, for once glad that I was on the other side of the castle from the Mullers. I got Enid to unlace my dress then I lay down on my bed to recover. Despite refusing as much food as I could without appearing rude, I felt full to bursting. I chuckled to think of Rory having to deal with the overindulging Bertram. I trusted him to get Bertram in a fit state for his dance with his brother's new wife. If he didn't, the results could be catastrophic. I chuckled again thinking of Rory's struggles and my stomach spasmed. I groaned. I reached out and rang the bell, in need of a soothing cup of tea, but long before Enid returned with it I had fallen into a deep sleep.

In fact, it wasn't until the bells began to ring that I woke at all.

CHAPTER
TWENTY

Euphemia is unlaced

My immediate reaction was one of confusion. Myriad bells were ringing, and not in harmony. However, I felt sure that Richard and Lucinda had returned from the church. Had I dreamed the wedding breakfast? My curtains were drawn, but Enid, as ever, must have been hurrying, for there was a slit through which a rosy light shone. I wondered if I had slept through the whole night. The bells continued to ring loudly and my head throbbed. Rising as I was from a dream state, and with so much cacophony, I found it hard to think clearly.

I slipped from my bed and discovered I was still dressed for dinner, but my laces were loose. I held up my dress front and stumbled over to the window. Drawing back the curtains, I beheld the cause of the warm light and it was as if I had been doused in ice water, for I was immediately awake. "Fire!" I screamed. "Fire!"

Below, one of the outbuildings blazed. Already a line of men passed buckets and threw water onto the fire, but the blaze appeared not in the least troubled by their efforts. The flames leapt high into the night, illuminating the courtyard and the people scurrying to and fro below. As my mind tried to function, I realised

138

some of the men carried shovels and that others were already digging. It took me a moment to understand. They were digging a ditch in the hope the fire would not cross it. They, too, appreciated that their efforts could not stop the flames, but were striving to keep the fire from reaching the castle. My one consolation was that little Amy was with her mother on the other side of the castle and so apparently in no immediate danger. As Lucinda was presumably with Richard, I knew only of Mary Hill who could still be on that floor of the tower. I opened the window and a cloud of smoke blew in, covering me in soot. I choked and coughed. Even at this distance, with the window open, the heat drove me back into the room. If the men did not get the ditch done in time, my tower would certainly be in danger. That is, if it had not already caught below, a nasty little voice whispered at the back of my mind. Could that be why no one had come to warn me? Was I already cut off?

I coughed some more, wracking spasms that brought me to my knees. Why would they still be digging the ditch if the fire was behind them? Or was everyone dancing? Dancing in the firelight? No, silly, a voice at the back of my mind said, they think you are downstairs with the others who are dancing. No one has remembered you are up here. A tear rolled down my face. I would die up here, forgotten, roasting slowly like an excess of chicken at a banquet.

It was an undignified situation. Without doubt, the best thing I could do was lie down on the extremely comfortable carpet — why had I never noticed it was so comfortable before? — and have a nice nap. When I woke up everything would be over. That annoying voice at the back of my mind shrieked at me not to lose consciousness, but I was quite certain I had already lost my grip on reality when the door burst open, and Bertram, his hair on end and his face covered in grime, stormed into the room.

My eyes fluttered open. I lay on a settee in the downstairs room where the Staplefords had held their family council. My head ached abominably and the tartan covers did nothing to help. Richenda's voice said, "Honestly, Euphemia, if you must make a spectacle of yourself do try and make sure your dress is properly fastened. When Bertram carried you out into the courtyard you caused quite a commotion."

I struggled to sit upright. My bodice and my person parted company. I caught the material to my front and blinked round at the room. "You could have fastened my dress," I said — or tried to say. My voice came out as a hoarse whisper and the effort of speaking the words cut into my throat like broken glass.

"There's only us in here," said Richenda. She stood by the window, looking out. I must have been asleep for some time, for the light outside had shifted from night to the greyness of dawn. "Besides, Mrs Lewis thought that as you had fainted we should leave it be. However, now you have regained consciousness I shall ring for a maid to aid you."

Two questions warred for prominence in my mind. "Are you cross and is the castle burnt?" I spoke as economically as I could.

"Why should I care?" said Richenda with a high little laugh. "It's not my castle."

I put my head back down on the pillow that someone thoughtful, presumably not Richenda, had put under my head. A cough spasmed through me, but it was nothing like the fit I had had in my bedchamber. It slowly occurred to me that in opening the window I had allowed my room to be overcome with smoke and in doing so half suffocated myself.

"You are very lucky to be alive," said Richenda, again with her increasingly uncanny ability to echo my thoughts.[1] "If Bertram had not seen you leaning out the window — although in your state of undress I imagine not a man in the courtyard missed you — you would have choked to death."

"Oh, dear God," I murmured. "How will I ever face anyone again?"

"You are covered in soot," said Richenda, "and besides, I do not believe anyone was looking at your face. If you are fortunate, no one will have recognised you." Then she sighed. "Provided Bertram can keep his valorous act to himself."

"Is he well?"

"The excitement of —" she looked me up and down, "seems to have quite bypassed his heart condition."

"Why the courtyard?" I gasped.

---

[1] If our situations had been somewhat different I might have remarked we were spending too much time together, but then that was my employ!

"Why indeed," said Richenda. "Hans had to help him carry you in here."

And there was the root of the trouble. Hans had seen me *en déshabillé*. "It must have been very dark," I croaked.

"Not with the firelight," snapped Richenda.

"I am sorry," I said as contritely as my injured voice would allow. Then, mercifully, Enid arrived to fasten my dress, wash the soot from my face, find me cushions to help me sit up, and even bring a drink of tea sweetened with honey to soothe my poor throat. During these ministrations Richenda kept her back firmly turned to me as she watched through the window. Once Enid had left I asked timidly. "What is happening?"

"One of little Lucinda's wedding presents has gone up in smoke," said Richenda. I waited for more information. "The outbuilding he was turning into a stable block for her is burnt out."

"But it did not reach the castle?"

"No," said Richenda. "You were never in danger. It seems the people here have learned their lesson from the last fire — or my brother, for once in his life, sought out decent advice. They knew exactly what to do in the case of fire."

"What started it?" I asked.

"No one knows," said Bertram, striding through the door. He wore no jacket and his shirt sleeves were rolled up. He was covered in grime, but grinning broadly. He took two quick steps and knelt by my side. "But you are safe."

"I believe I must thank you for my rescue," I said. The tea was helping my voice enormously. "You were quite the hero."

"And you were quite the idiot for opening the window," muttered Richenda. Bertram and I ignored her.

"I understand," I said blushing furiously, "that I was . . ."

Bertram raised an eyebrow. "That you were what, Euphemia?"

I cast my eyes down. "Not entirely respectable when you found me. I am very sorry."

"Oh, don't worry about that," said Bertram in an all too cheery voice. "Is that why Richenda is so upset? Honestly, everyone was looking at the fire, not you."

"Except for you and Hans," said Richenda.

"Well, Hans is a man of the world," said Bertram. "As am I." He turned his attention back to me. "But I am also a gentleman. And I assure you, Euphemia, I was more concerned for your safety than the state of your apparel. As I am sure was Muller."

Richenda snorted loudly.

"Oh come on, Richenda!" said Bertram. "I grant you it has all been a bit dramatic, but it is not as if anyone has died."

Hans entered the room as Bertram was offering this cheery opinion. His face, too, was covered in soot and his expression sombre. "I only wish you were correct, Bertram," he said sadly. "But two bodies have just been found in the ruins."

CHAPTER
TWENTY-ONE

Chief Inspector Stewart

The local constabulary were sent for and all the guests were requested to stay at the castle. For once, I felt I could retire to my room, which Enid had swept clean of soot, as I could not possibly have anything to do with this turn of events. I requested a light breakfast of toast and more tea with honey and prepared to spend the rest of the day in bed, recovering both my voice and my dignity. So I was somewhat surprised when Enid appeared around lunch time with a summons for me to speak to the Police Chief Inspector.

The Chief Inspector, a tall, rangy man with a remarkably thick and bristly blonde moustache, dressed in green tweed and with only a slight Scottish lilt to his accent, greeted me warily. He had set up his office in what was clearly intended to be a study. Although shelves lined the wall, they were only half full. A rather lovely rosewood desk had been dragged into the centre of the room. The Chief Inspector had been seated behind it on a grand carved chair, his sergeant on a plainer seat to his left, but he rose as I entered. "Miss St John, I presume?" he said in rather a gruff voice.

"Indeed, but I am at a loss . . ."

"Please." He indicated I should sit in a chair in front of the desk and sat down himself. He shuffled some papers on his desk and made a puffing noise into his moustache. "This is somewhat irregular, but Sir Richard has insisted that you are interviewed."

"I can hardly see why," I said as calmly as possible. Inside I was seething. Trust Stapleford to try and bring me into all this. "After the wedding breakfast I retired to my room — the maid Enid saw to me, and I remained there until I foolishly opened the window and was overcome by smoke. I am indebted to Mr Bertram Stapleford for saving me."

"We have heard about that incident from several sources," said the Chief Inspector. Behind him his sergeant obviously suppressed a snigger. I sat a little straighter in my chair and did my best to channel my mother's most disapproving demeanour.

"And?" I asked. "If you know I was in my room at the time of the fire, how can I possibly help you in your investigation?"

"It has been brought to our attention that you have been involved in several previous — er — suspicious demises."

"If you know that," I answered as cuttingly as I could, "then you will also know that at no time has any suspicion been cast upon me."

"We are awaiting confirmation about the incidents from head office," said the Chief Inspector, who huffed ferociously into his moustache again.

"Ah, I see," I said. "Someone has been casting aspersions. Do you have the offence of libel in Scotland?"

"Defamation," said the Chief Inspector shortly. "I am not suggesting that . . ."

"But someone else is," I said baldly.

The Chief Inspector sat back in his chair. "I am afraid, ma'am, that you are not at all what I was led to believe. Shall we start again, Miss St John? I am Chief Inspector Robert Stewart from Inverness, and I have been charged with investigating this situation. I am not familiar with either the current inhabitants of the castle or the previous owners, who I believe are also on the premises. I am, therefore, somewhat over-reliant on what supposedly respectable members of this establishment have told me."

"Sir Richard told you that I cause trouble," I surmised. "And despite the fact there is nothing to link me to last night's occurrence, he has insisted you interview me — and considering that as well as holding a minor title he is also an MP, you felt it would do no harm to comply. In fact, you might also have felt it would harm the helpfulness of the — er — locals if you did not comply. Plus, if you are anything like your sergeant, you may also have been curious."

At this, the sergeant turned a satisfactory shade of beetroot. The Chief Inspector turned and muttered something sharp under his breath to the sergeant. Then he turned back to me. "Yes, not at all what I was led to expect," he repeated. "You assess the situation admirably, ma'am. You are quite correct in thinking I would have ruled you completely out of the investigation if there had not been whispers about your previous adventures, and if you had not decided to miss the wedding ceremony. You must admit it sits oddly that one would travel all this way only to forgo the wedding itself."

"But surely Mrs Muller has explained?"

"Mrs Muller currently feels unable to answer questions, and as she is in a delicate situation . . ."

"And has recently fallen down the stairs and sprained her ankle," I broke in. "And was thus unable to walk to the church along with everyone else. I, as her companion, stayed behind."

Stewart huffed several times into his moustache before saying, "That would account for it, yes. Will Mrs Muller be able to confirm that you did not leave her side at any point? Only we have a witness who places you on the ground floor, near the main entrance, when the wedding party returned."

"I left her when we heard the bells celebrating the wedding. She wished to quickly bathe and change her dress."

"You did not stay to help her?"

"I am a companion, not a maid," I said icily.

"Forgive me. I am not intimately acquainted with the duties of a companion. I had thought they were a relic of the older generation. Mrs Muller's husband is still alive, is he not?"

"Yes, and often working away from home in the City for days at a time. His estate is in the country."

"And this is where you reside with his wife and . . ." he rifled through some papers, "his adopted daughter. A strange fancy to adopt a child when he has a wife able to bear him children."

"That is the Mullers' business and of no bearing to the current situation."

"That we shall see. I understand that the Stapleford seat is bequeathed to whichever of the Stapleford heirs first has legitimate offspring. Which would be your employer, Mrs Muller, yes?"

"And she has given away that right to Sir Richard as a wedding gift to him and his bride."

"Very thoughtful, I am sure, but that leaves Mr . . . ," he searched through his papers some more. "Mr Bertram Stapleford."

I looked at him blankly. How could we have missed this? Richenda forgoing her right in law did not automatically mean Bertram had forgone his. "Bertram is unmarried," I said.

"A state I am sure the gentleman could rectify if he wished. I believe he has an extensive estate in Norfolk?"

I thought of the sinking monstrosity that Bertram called home, but instinct warned me not give away how well I knew it. Fitzroy would never have given away information so freely. The Chief Inspector was throwing out lures left and right, probing for something, anything to latch onto. I would have to guard my temper and ensure that I was not the lead he decided to follow. I did not feel particularly alarmed as I had nothing to do with current events, but neither did I wish to be dragged into another murder. Even I felt it was becoming far too habitual.

"Have you been aware of anything unusual happening at the castle?"

"I have only been here four days," I responded. "I do not know what is usual in this part of the world."

"For Scotland?" asked the Chief Inspector.

"I meant for the current environs," I said. "The castle and the staff are mostly new to me."

"Mostly?"

"I have previously met Mrs Lewis," I conceded.

"Ah, yes, Mrs Lewis. The housekeeper who was here when the castle had the previous, more disastrous fire." I heard the note of self-congratulation in his voice. He had linked me with the previous fire.

"Indeed, I believe it happened long before we met."

"And how did you meet, exactly?"

"In working for the Mullers, when circumstances required we return to Stapleford Hall, shortly after which I met Mrs Lewis."

"At a previous New Year celebration, I believe?"

"If you knew that, why ask?" I snapped.

"I have also been informed that you have spent some time in prison under suspicion of arson."

At this point I thought of Fitzroy again, but in the most unladylike terms. I thought how I would dearly like to shake hands with his neck. My time in prison had been in service to the Nation, but I was bound by the Official Secrets Act from revealing any details. I could only hope that if I was arrested, Fitzroy, if he was even in the country, would hear about it and come to my aid.

"I was released without charge," I said. I determined to keep my answers from now on both simple and true. It had not for a moment occurred to me that anyone

149

would know about the arson episode, let alone bring it up at this time. Stapleford. I knew it was Stapleford. I doubted he thought I had set the fire, but he hated me enough to, at the very least, create an uncomfortable situation for me.

"Are you a member of the WSPU?"

"No," I said. It had never occurred to me to subscribe despite supporting their objectives. I swore internally to remedy this situation once we were back in England.

"You just fancied a bit of an outing?"

"You are correct in assuming I was caught up in the march by accident," I said calmly. "I was accompanying Mrs Muller to the capital for a spot of shopping and sightseeing." I made a mental note to ensure Richenda did not contradict me. It would be in her best interests not to do so.

"I see," said Stewart. He produced a pencil from his pocket and made a side note in the margin of one of his pieces of paper. This was accompanied with more blowing into his moustache. I wondered if anyone had ever told him what an unattractive habit it was. His age could be anywhere between thirty and fifty, but I would have laid odds there was no Mrs Stewart. What wife would put up with all that panting and puffing?

"I said, was there anything you wished to add?"

I jerked my attention away from the repellent moving hairs on his face. "Do you know who the bodies in the building are?"

"I was thinking more along the lines of you offering me information," retorted the Chief Inspector, who it seemed did possess a modicum of humour under all that facial hair. "But I see no harm in telling you what is known by every single groundsman. One of the bodies was found curled up, obviously overcome by smoke, but still reasonably intact given the ferocity of the fire. A man, not young, but not particularly old either. Possibly a passing tramp who sought shelter on the wrong night. The other is more problematic. A skeleton revealed when a wall fell during the fire. The local doctor believes it to be of a woman. We assume she must have been there for some time."

My surprise must have shown on my face.

"Did you assume it was someone else, Miss St John?"

"I really had no idea, Chief Inspector. But to find one recent body and one skeleton does seem rather excessive."

The sergeant suppressed another snigger, but this time it was not at my expense.

"I believe that will be all, Miss St John," said Stewart. I rose and was halfway to the door before he added, "At least for now."

CHAPTER
TWENTY-TWO

Mary is blackmailed

Much like a wounded animal, my initial response was to retreat to my room, but it occurred to me that I was not the only resident who had been locked up for suspected arson. I went in search of Mary Hill. I found her in her room reading a book on socialism. She was at some pains to ensure I saw the title.

"And so you see," I finished, "I thought I should warn you."

Mary gazed at me levelly. "Did you inform the Inspector that I was in the cell with you?" she enquired.

"No, of course not."

"Unless you have shared that information with anyone present here I doubt it will have reached the Inspector's ears. The information was never circulated in the papers or I would have been in trouble with the Dean of my college. It seems you have made an enemy of someone among us. Who here knew of your incarceration?"

"My employer Richenda, her husband Hans, and her stepbrother Bertram Stapleford."

"Ah, yes, the man you claimed as your brother, or was it your fiancé? You told so many misleading *histories* it is somewhat difficult to keep track of the truth."

"I know I deserve that," I said, pushing down my temper, "but you must understand that everything I did was in cause of rooting out the murderer."

"Which at one point you believed to be me? I don't believe they did ever arrest anyone, did they?"

Oh, how I hated the Official Secrets Act with a passion. I had, in fact, solved this murder, but I could not risk telling Mary without revealing my association with the British Secret Service — or whatever Fitzroy was calling himself now. I swallowed down my bile. "No, they did not."

"And you were, in fact, entirely wrong?" persisted Mary.

"It would appear so," I said through gritted teeth.

"Or it was all a rather clever charade to cover your own actions!"

I gaped at her. I stood dumbstruck for a few moments before I exploded, "I have never killed anyone!"

"Ah, finally," said Mary, "the sound of truth. Well, neither have I. So, as long as none of your associates mention my name in connection with our previous association, I imagine I will shortly be allowed to leave."

I was about to protest but, in truth, the woman owed me no favours. "I will keep my counsel on one condition," I said, thinking quickly.

Mary raised an eyebrow. "So now you enter into the murky depths of blackmail?"

"I will keep your secret if you will agree to meet me at a time of mutual convenience in London for afternoon tea."

Whatever Mary had expected me to say, it was not this. "Why?" she asked, her mathematical mind cutting directly to the heart of the problem.

"Because I think we have begun on the wrong foot. We are not so dissimilar, you and I, and I would like the chance to prove it to you."

"Well, you have some nerve," said Mary. "I will give you that." She stood frowning for a few moments. I waited. I did not feel that saying anything else would help. Finally, she spoke. "I accept. We shall communicate by telegram and arrange a suitable meeting date in the New Year." She handed me her card. "That is if you are not in jail by then." Then she picked up her book once more and began to read. It was clear that I was dismissed.

I left the room and slowly made my way down to the ground floor of the castle. I was not yet sure where I was going. I regretted that Mary and I still stood on such bad terms. She had a quick and precise mind that I knew would have been of help untangling the current problem. However, she had shown no interest in the matter beyond not being falsely accused. (Again.) Was this, I wondered, how real ladies thought? To all others, with the exception of my strange small band of friends, was crime something best either swept under the carpet or left to the police service?[1]

I turned a corner and began ascending the stairs to the Mullers' suite. If nothing else, I should enquire after Richenda's health. Perhaps if I told her of my interview with the Chief Inspector she would be so interested she would forget to be angry with me. Richenda had proven to be of great use in the arson case, much to everyone's surprise. She was not as unobservant as was commonly thought. She had realised quite some time ago that Bertram and I had "adventures", even if she had no idea that we were more and more often forced into these due to the "security of the nation". She had also felt very much left out. Yes, definitely involving her now would help ease her moods and who was to say her unique outlook might not shed some light on the problem at hand. If only she was not with . . .

I opened the door to her suite and saw her sitting with her husband. Hans rose at once and came over to me. "My dear Euphemia, you look pale. Are you sure it is wise to be up and walking around so soon after your misadventure?"

---

[1] It depends on where you stand on the social scale. If you are important enough in the Empire then your misdemeanours, however bad, will inevitably be swept under the red, white and blue rug. However, if you are poor and have stolen a loaf of bread, prepare for the harshest sentence the law can invoke. Justice is meant to be blind, but in His Majesty's United Kingdom of Great Britain and Ireland, that blindfold seems to slip all too often.

I could have happily slapped him. For an intelligent man, Hans sometimes displays no understanding of his wife: she was throwing daggers with her eyes at me from behind him.

I had no option. I said, "I have just been interviewed by the police. They have learned I was arrested on suspicion of arson previously and I believe I am now what is called 'a person of interest in their enquiries'."

Hans turned to face his wife. "Oh no," said Richenda. "I didn't. I did not mention a word to anyone."

"I am sure you did not," I said, sitting down on a chair with an uncomfortable thud, the cushion being more for design than comfort. "I imagine the only person who would wish me so ill is Richard."

"But how would he know?" asked Richenda.

"He is a man with connections," I said, shrugging.

"I don't see how," began Hans, when Bertram entered the room.

"What ho!" he said. "Another murder. Euphemia, you really are an albatross; certainly livened up Richard's wedding, though. I passed him in the Great Hall. He is spitting feathers! No doubt he thought he'd be lying late in bed with his new wife this morning, instead he's ..." he stopped and took in our expressions. "Why are you looking at me like that?" he said, suspicion and wariness seeping into his voice.

"Mystery solved," said Richenda.

"I do not think, my dear ..." interjected Hans diplomatically.

156

"You know what he is like when he has a drink in him," said Richenda. "And of late that has been happening far too often for my liking."

"Are you talking about me?" blustered Bertram. "I own I like a glass or two of port after dinner, but no more than the next man."

"I would not be surprised if Bertram, with another glass of port and a cigar, was not responsible for this whole sad affair," opined Richenda, who then promptly burst into tears.

CHAPTER
TWENTY-THREE

Unlucky for some

As one, Bertram and I backed out of the room. "Pregnant women say all sorts of things they do not mean," I said gently. "She is overwrought."

"Walk in the grounds with me?" asked Bertram.

I stopped only to pick up my hat and coat before accompanying him outside. The air was as sharp as a knife against our skins, cold and bitter, but the noonday sun shone brightly. "Happy New Year," said Bertram, and kissed me quickly on the cheek.

"Good heavens," I said. "I had quite forgotten. So this is 1913."

"Another year, another murder," said Bertram gloomily. "My life certainly has changed since I met you, Euphemia."

"I wish you would stop saying that. It is much more to do with your brother than it is to do with me."

"Hmm," said Bertram, extending a hand to help me over a particularly rough patch. "I suspect it is also that I didn't notice these things much before. I mean, if I'd tripped over a dead body I'm certain I would have said something like, 'Look, a dead body!' and toddled off to telephone the police —"

"Which is more than some members of the upper classes would do."

"Thank you, Euphemia. But, the thing is, after doing that I would not have given it any more thought. Unless, of course, it was someone I knew well. In which case, I would have felt rather sad." His gaze fixed on the path before us and he sank into his thoughts. I left a silence between us for a while, and we walked on, admiring the magnificent and wild scenery that the Highlands spread before us. The castle grounds were nestled in a valley, or glen, as the Scotch call them, and on three sides mountains rose to snowy peaks, their sides dressed in an interwoven hoard of trees of every description. There was little in the way of formal gardens. Instead, the lawn and gravelled driveway gave way to fields. The land here was flat enough that we could make out the village huddled at the foot of a mountain in the distance. Between the castle and this lay fields of cattle: sheep, cows and goats, all puffing a heavy cloud of vapour into the cold air. I wondered what the beasts had made of the wedding procession. The ground was set hard under foot, so walking was easy enough.

I had no difficulty being silent with Bertram. We had grown easy in each other's company, but I could not help feeling guilty. Eventually I said, "I do understand what you mean. I had a conversation with Mary Hill earlier today that made me realise how very different I am to most women." I then related our conversation. At the end of it, Bertram stopped and grabbed both my hands.

"That's not what I meant at all. I do not regret how you have opened my eyes to the reality of justice. Or, should I say, the reality of the lack of justice in this world." He let go of my hands to wipe his hand over his forehead. "For the life of me I cannot work out where it goes wrong. As children we are taught right from wrong, but then, as we emerge into adulthood, my class at least seems to believe it is somehow above these values we were taught to hold dear as children — simply because we have money and position. Before I met you, Euphemia, I never thought about it. I never even noticed and now I cannot stop noticing."

I swallowed hard. Feelings came so swiftly I could barely name them. "I am glad, of course I am glad," I said, "that you wish to strive against injustice, but I wonder how much of a good turn I have done you. In so many instances when we have come across wrongs those responsible have been left unpunished."

"But not always," said Bertram. "I know in the scheme of things we are both but small creatures, but I think it is important that we strive to see that right is done. One man — or woman — campaigning may not be of significance alone, but with each person, each voice, strength is gathered. Justice calls us and we have heard. We can only hope that more and more will heed her voice and that one day we will be a land of the just."

I thought this was getting a bit melodramatic, even for Bertram, who can be abnormally sensitive at times, but I could not mock his sentiments. Indeed, I found myself blinking back a tear or two at his sincerity.

160

"But do you know what I really need now?" asked Bertram, with great seriousness.

"What?"

"A buttered muffin."

I burst out laughing. Bertram grinned ruefully. "It's damnably cold out here, Euphemia, and a man must eat."

We made our way back towards the house in much higher spirits than the occasion warranted. Bertram took my coat and handed it to a footman. "I would not concern yourself, Euphemia," he said. "I think the Chief Inspector was merely trying to rattle you. I doubt he seriously entertains any thoughts that you might be responsible. I mean, anyone looking at you would know at once that you were not an arsonist. Besides, Hans, Richie and myself will all vouch for you."

"I am not so sure about Richenda," I said.

"Ah," said Bertram with a sly grin. "The incident with the dress. She is making more of it than there was to — er — see."

"I would rather not discuss the matter," I said stiffly. Bertram flashed me a grin and I shook my head at him. In good accord, we made our way back to the Mullers' suite. Bertram pulled a wary face at me, his hand on the latch. We listened for a moment and heard only a low murmur of voices. "Doesn't sound too heated," he said. "I reckon Richie has either calmed down or gone to lie down." He opened the door. We walked in to see Richenda rise to her feet and say, "You wish to interview my servants?" in outraged tones that would have done credit to a Duchess. Standing implacably in front of her was Chief Inspector Stewart.

"If you do not object, ma'am," he said. "And even if you do, I am afraid I must insist."

"Well, honestly!" said Richenda, turning to Hans for support.

Hans shrugged. "We only have two servants with us, Chief Inspector, a nursery maid, Mrs Susie Ellis, and my brother-in-law brought his servant, Mr Rory McLeod." He spotted us behind Stewart. "You don't object to the police interrogating McLeod, do you, Bertram?" Then, without waiting for a response, he continued, "As you will have discovered, my other brother-in-law, Sir Richard, has a superfluity of servants, so it was quite unnecessary to bring them up from our estates. Things get to a ridiculous state when servants outnumber guests by more than five to one, wouldn't you agree, Chief Inspector?" Hans' tone was polite and amicable, but it was clear he was reminding the Chief Inspector that he was among his betters.

I had taken Stewart in some dislike, but I was impressed when he stood his ground and repeated his request. Hans pulled the bell. He also suggested Richenda retire. "My wife is expecting our first child and I do not wish her to be disturbed by this unfortunate incident. However, I am certain you will understand that Bertram and myself will stay while you speak with our people." Richenda looked none too pleased at being dismissed. I did my best to melt into the background, so no one would suggest I, too, was removed from the room. However, the Chief Inspector

162

knew how to play his cards and did not fruitlessly protest at witnesses to his interviews. Instead, when the servant arrived to carry the messages to Rory and Ellie, he merely asked that she also locate his sergeant and direct the man to join us.

Rory appeared first. "I understand you are a socialist with Bolshevik sympathies," said the Chief Inspector before he was even halfway into the room.

"Bloody Richard!" ejaculated Bertram. "That's where all this nonsense is coming from. Why is he trying to blame us for what happened?"

"I am afraid that your brother loses rationality when angry," replied Hans evenly.

Stewart looked between them, frowning. Rory spoke up, "I have, in the past, joined a form of socialist movement, sir. My membership was short lived. I was much younger and very much in love with a girl who was extremely keen on politics."

"Do you still see her?" asked the Chief Inspector.

"I have no idea where she is and, truthfully, barely remember her name. I was not exactly thinking with my brain during my youth, sir!"

I caught Hans looking over at me to see if I was shocked. I decided to find the ceiling very interesting.

"And the time you were arrested for murder?"

"I was incarcerated in a kitchen cupboard for a short period of time and released when the real culprit was apprehended. If you wish for a character reference from outside this room you may approach the Earl of (here he mentioned a friend of my grandfather) for whom I butlered for a short time when his own man was indisposed, and with whom I have a standing invitation to return to his employ."

"You do? said Bertram, startled.

"I do not like being played for a fool," said the Chief Inspector darkly.

"He is connected to the telephone system, as, I believe, is this castle. You can ring him or send a telegram. I am certain he will confirm what I have said."

The Chief Inspector harrumphed into his moustache. Just then, his sergeant entered and he berated him, in language I will not repeat, for his tardiness.

"Stewart! Ladies present!" cried Bertram.

The Chief Inspector appeared to notice me for the first time. "You should not be here," he said.

"I am staying to chaperone Miss Ellis," I said, inspiration striking me so that I conveniently forgot she was *Mrs* Ellis.[1]

The Chief Inspector made another loud and unpleasant puffing noise. Then he commanded his sergeant to take Rory aside and get a short statement from him about his whereabouts during the time around the fire, while we waited for Ellie to appear.

By the time Ellie arrived, Rory had finished. He walked towards the door. "Not yet," said the Chief Inspector sharply. "I want you and Miss Ellis to have a look at this and tell me if you recognise it. It was found on the burned body in the outbuilding." I peered over

[1] Of course, a married woman would not have needed a chaperone.

164

his shoulder, struggling to make out the small object. It was a tie-pin with a horseshoe design, sooty from the fire, but a glint of gold shone through. There appeared to be a tiny diamond set at the bottom of the horseshoe. I edged in carefully, trying to see more clearly, when there was a heavy thud beside me. I turned to find that at the sight of the tie-pin Ellie had dropped into a dead faint.

CHAPTER
TWENTY-FOUR

A remarkable confession

Immediately there was a commotion, as there can be only when a room full of men find themselves with a fainting female.[1] The sergeant, being the most practical of the lot, removed the flowers from a vase on the mantelpiece and dashed the water in the unfortunate maid's face. She came round coughing and spluttering. I knelt down beside her and helped her to her feet. Hans rose from the sofa and together we laid her out on it. I heard Rory mutter to Bertram, "That looked like the real thing."

Stewart grunted and huffed and swore at his sergeant. Then he turned his attention to Ellie. "That was an extraordinary reaction, Miss Ellis. Can you explain yourself?"

"I say, Chief Inspector!" protested Bertram.

"The girl is not herself," said Hans.

Rory said nothing. I waited to see how Ellie would react. She fluttered her damp lashes. Tears began to

---

[1] As this appears to be a frequent occurrence in drawing rooms, one might have assumed they would, by now, have worked out what to do. But no. The sight of one fainting woman and the males of our species appear to lose their wits.

course silently down her face and her breath caught in sobs.

"Miss Ellis, I must press you," said Stewart.

Bertram burst out in protest again.[1] Rory and I exchanged glances.

Eventually the girl got control of herself. "It is nothing," she said. "I am very silly, but you did say this was found on a dead man. A man burned alive." She shivered. "You will think me superstitious, but I am a little afraid of such an unlucky object."

"More unlucky for the chap who wore it," muttered Rory under his breath. I sneaked a side on glance at his face. He was frowning and not looking particularly sympathetic. Rory is an excellent reader of character and I knew he had had qualms about Ellie from the start, but would a woman set a fire? It would be an easier way for her to kill than attempting to stick a knife into a man, but why would she do it? We had brought her up from England. Could she know anyone up here? I realised we knew very little about Ellie. While the men hovered uncertainly around her, I tiptoed out of the room and made my way down to the room where I knew the telephonic apparatus to be. I hated the things, but I needed to speak to Hans' butler, Stone. With luck, I would be able to find that nice footman, Rupert, to help me.

----

[1] He is forever taking the side of what he perceives as vulnerable females. It is most annoying and frequently lands him in more hot water than he can handle!

I returned a little time later having given Stone my instructions, which he had been somewhat reluctant to carry out. It had taken all my persuasive skills to get him to act. The scene in the room I had left had changed. Ellie was gone. Hans was absent, but now Richenda had rejoined us. But, most startling of all, Mrs Lewis stood in the middle of the room, obviously in mid-appeal to the others.

Hans nodded at me to come into the room. The housekeeper continued.

"I need your help," said Mrs Lewis, her craggy features as pitiful as any gargoyle's in my late father's church. "It's true. I was here when it happened."

"Good God!" exclaimed Bertram. "And Stapleford still hired you?"

"Don't be dense, man," said Rory, with an extreme lack of regard for his employer's status. "You never told him, did you?"

"No," said Mrs Lewis, and, to my shock, she burst into tears. "This accursed place," she said. "It brings nothing but unhappiness."

"You have been accused? For once," I said, "it would have been nice to attend a party without complications."

"Then you should not have come to work for my family," said my employer Richenda Muller. She then burped loudly, and sat down. "Sorry all," she said without a blush, "that just keeps happening." And then she did something no lady ever should do, as her nether regions echoed her previous respiratory efforts. Instead of rushing from the room in shame, Richenda laughed

168

loudly. But then what can you expect of a woman whose best friend until her marriage was a horse?

Rory, with the disdain of a perfect servant, did not turn a hair. Bertram, on the other hand, choked. "Good God!" he exclaimed. "For the love of God, please Richenda, never eat haggis again."

"Please," I said, "can we be serious? If I am right we may have a lynch mob at the gates any moment." Rory's handsome face went pale and Bertram, ever a martyr to his blood pressure, turned an unbecoming puce. Richenda, in alarm, again broke wind from both ends. She turned on me, demanding, "How on Earth do you keep being dragged into situations like this, Euphemia!"

As she is my employer, I could not retort that in fact, this time, the cause of our situation could be laid at her husband's door. Bertram voiced my thoughts. "If it hadn't been for your husband's insistence, I would have been quite happy in spending New Year in my own home, waterlogged though it may be!"

"And miss your brother's wedding?" asked Rory, surprised.

Bertram did not bother to speak. The look he gave Rory spoke volumes. "Aye, well, I guess yous are not close," commented Rory, slipping slightly into Scotch as he tends to do under stressful circumstances.

"For the sake of expediency," I said, cutting through the chatter, "can you please confirm, on your honour, Mrs Lewis, that you did not set this fire?"

"I did not," said Mrs Lewis in a composed manner.

"And the previous fire under the last Laird's ownership?"

"I do not see how that is relevant," said Mrs Lewis.

"What!" exclaimed Rory. "You did set that one?"

"I have no comment to make on the subject," said the housekeeper, sitting very straight in her chair.

Richenda cocked her head to one side. "Oh, I know this game. Richard used to make me do this when I was little." She turned to look at Bertram. "He must have tried it on you too, Bertie. You know he'd have done something naughty, like broken a vase or killed one of the house dogs . . ."

"Killed a dog!" I interjected, surprised.

"Oh, he killed two — at least, I think," said Richenda blithely. "He said it was an accident, but now — well, you have to wonder."

"Sounds like the man was always a monster," said Rory.

"Yes, never mind that," said the single-minded Richenda. "We are talking about Mrs Lewis."

"I thought you were talking about Richard," said Bertram, bemused. "Has she killed a dog too? Only I am rather fond of dogs and I wouldn't want . . ."

"Shut up, Bertie," said Richenda. "She hasn't killed any animals except the odd chicken."

"Chickens are quite sweet really," said Bertram.

"Yes," said Richenda pointedly. "Especially in stew."

"Oh, I see what you mean," said Bertram, "but you said . . ."

I felt like covering my ears to block out their bickering. I could feel a blistering rebuke building

170

inside me when Richenda continued, "I was trying to say that when Richard did not want to take the blame for something, he used to persuade me to refuse to say I hadn't done it."

"How did he pay you?" asked Bertram. "In cake?"

"Cake at first. Later, threats," said Richenda darkly, "but you see my point. Mrs Lewis is protecting someone."

I spent a moment joining up the mental dots only to realise that, despite her seemingly inane chatter, Richenda had provided a worthy insight. Especially as I perceived that Mrs Lewis had begun to redden. Even more strange was that Rory had moved silently to the back of the room and appeared to be sidling towards the exit. Rory has made the study of butlering his whole world for several years and has nigh on perfected the butler's silent glide, despite his tall frame, but someone who is ever conscious of his presence cannot slip away quite so easily as he might do with the master of the house. "Rory," I said sharply. "Where are you going?"

"If Mr Bertram is going to attend dinner tonight, it is time for me to draw his bath."

"I think we have more important matters on our minds than Bertie's bath," said Richenda.

"Indeed," I echoed. "One might almost think this discussion of baths was a smoke-screen." I admit it was an unfortunate turn of phrase, but I was distracted.

"Could you please stop talking about my bath as if I am a toddler?" exclaimed Bertram. "I am still in the room and I do *not* require a bath!"

171

"Forgive my saying so, sir. But it is vitally important to bathe before dining."

"I don't see Richie's or Euphemia's maids here bleating about baths," said Bertram. "Or are you suggesting I am particularly grubby!"

"I am suggesting that your valet-butler is attempting to leave the room before Mrs Lewis is forced into admitting who she is protecting."

Mrs Lewis' lips set in a grim line.

Rory's shoulders sagged. "You might as well admit it, Mrs Lewis," he said. "I gave my word I would not tell on you, but it seems to me like they already know."

Mrs Lewis gave a huge sigh. Then she said, "Yes, I set the fire."

CHAPTER
TWENTY-FIVE

Richenda's rare insight

"This one or the original?" asked Bertram with remarkable calm.

"The original one," said Mrs Lewis. "You have my word I have nothing to do with the more recent conflagration."

"Why?" asked Bertram.

"I prefer not to say," said Mrs Lewis.

"I don't believe her," said Richenda. "I still say she's covering for someone."

Rory shook his head. "Leave it, Richenda. She did it. I have information from a reliable source."

"A source?" asked Bertram. "Who?"

"I am not at liberty to say, sir."

"That's ridiculous," said Richenda. "You don't know the people up here anymore than we do. Unless you have recently become involved with someone — and even if you had, why should she know about Mrs Lewis? Were you seen?" She directed the last half of her query at the beleaguered housekeeper.

"No, I was not."

"You are very sure about that?" I said.

Mrs Lewis inclined her head.

"And yet, Rory has met someone who knows you started that fire all those years ago. I don't believe you have left the castle, except to go to the garage, since we have been here, Rory, and you would hardly be dallying with a woman old enough to remember the fire, so . . ."

"Leave it, Euphemia," said Rory roughly.

"I am right!" cried Richenda triumphantly. "Don't you see — neither of them did it!" We all looked at her blankly. "Oh come on!" said Richenda. "You're meant to be the brainy ones. Bertram, you remember when you were seven and you broke Mama's pink vase? And Richard and I got the blame?"

Bertram stuck a finger under his collar and tugged. "Ah, yes, shouldn't have done that. Wasn't cricket."

"Richard was even more beastly to me than usual for weeks, because he thought I'd done it and I thought he'd done it. It was ages before we worked it out."

"That was why you cut up Bumble!"

"Who the hel — heck is Bumble?" said Rory.

"My teddy bear," said Bertram. "Or he was. Do you mean Mrs Lewis had been duped?"

"Finally," said Richenda, giving a little whoop. "She is protecting someone *she* thinks did it, but from what Rory says, whoever is his source thinks Mrs Lewis herself did it!"

"So?" said Bertram.

"Neither of them did it," I said.

"Exactly," said Richenda.

"But who is your source, Rory?"

"It can only be whoever Mrs Lewis is trying to protect," said Richenda.

Mrs Lewis turned pure white and grasped at her throat. "No," she whispered. "No, he died." And then she slid from her chair in a dead faint.

"Her husband," said Bertram.

"Aye," said Rory. "Give me a hand to get her back on her seat, man! I've had my fill of fainting women today."

"But how do you know him?" asked Richenda. "Is he a relative?"

"Not all Scots are related," said Rory sourly.

"Oh, good heavens," I said, making a startling leap. "It cannot be the tramp? The man the Highlanders thought was a German spy?"

"What are you talking about?" snapped Richenda. "I thought I'd made a breakthrough and now you're spouting nonsense about Germans. If you are about to accuse my Hans —"

"No," said Rory. "When Euphemia and I were up in the Highlands minding the Stapleford Lodge staff for Bertram, you remember?"

"Someone drowned in a loch?"

"Yes, but that's not the important bit," I said. Bertram gave me a rather shocked look. "There was a man the locals kept seeing — well, not seeing, but seeing evidence of. They made up quite a lot of stories about him and we did think for a while —" I caught Bertram's eye. "Yes, well never mind that. Rory came and told me one evening that we didn't need to worry about who or what he was. That was because you had met him, wasn't it?"

"Her husband," said Richenda in a revelatory voice.

"I said that," said Bertram, sounding irked.

"Aye, he was the butler here at the time of the fire. He thought she had set the fire, by accident mind — and she obviously thought he had done it."

"But why . . ." I began.

"He's even more disfigured than she is, Euphemia," said Rory. "He wanted her to remember him the way he was, so he let her believe him dead. He was in hospital for a long time; sent far away to get his burns treated, unconscious. There was so much going on that night that when he woke up they had to ask him his name. He realised he was far away from the castle, so he gave them a false name. But years later, when he heard she was working for the Staplefords, he couldn't resist trying to take a peek at her. Still loved her, o' course. But he thought he was protecting her. Only she never came up to the lodge. It was I who found him."

"And you never said a word?" asked Bertram.

"It wasnae relevant to anything we were doing and, besides, the man had his pride."

"It's not like she's much of a looker herself," said Richenda. "Was it the fire that made her that way?"

"Aye, and him too," said Rory, "carrying her out of the burning building."

"That's tragically romantic," I said.

"It also means that neither of them were reasonable, then or now," said Bertram.

Mrs Lewis stirred. "My bath," said Bertram.

"Indeed sir," said Rory and both men bailed on us, leaving us to explain to the now-conscious Mrs Lewis that not only was her husband not dead, but neither was he an arsonist.

CHAPTER
TWENTY-SIX

Richenda does it again

After dinner, during which I pettily refused to pass Bertram the bread rolls, no matter how many times he looked mournfully at me, Richenda, Bertram and I adjourned to our favourite small sitting room. This time Hans accompanied us. Mrs Lewis was, of course, needed below stairs. It transpired that although the Chief Inspector had told her not to leave the castle, he had yet to actually arrest her.

"The man is clearly throwing out accusations left and right to try and stir us all up," said Rory.

"And darling Richard has been helping him along," said Richenda. "Euphemia, it is safe for Amy to be with Ellie, isn't it?"

I hesitated.

"No lynch mobs at the door yet, Euphemia?" broke in Bertram, who was clearly still smarting from the lack of dinner rolls he had consumed.

"I think we need to speak to my maid, Enid," I said. "And perhaps her grandmother."

"What on earth are you gabbling about?" said Richenda rudely.

"I think Euphemia has been doing some stirring-up of her own," said Hans with a smile.

"Oh, do you know who did it?" asked Richenda eagerly.

I shook my head. "What I know doesn't make sense, but I will be happy to share it with you. From what I've understood there were two bodies found, but only one was recent?"

Hans nodded. "Once we had you safe I went back out to see what I could do to help."

"It was Hans' idea to dig the ditch," said Richenda proudly.

"It is a common way to contain fires. I am surprised it is not known up here," Hans said.

"Too damn wet in this country," said Bertram, earning himself a scowl from Rory.

"From what you have described there were a great many people panicking. It appears the previous fire was within recent memory?" I asked.

"About five years ago, from what the servants say," said Rory.

I considered. "I could still be right."

"About what?" asked Bertram irritably.

"Two things. I was thinking that with so recent and devastating a fire awakening old memories — or not so old ones — the locals and staff may have been liable to panic until they received clear direction." I nodded at Hans. "The other guests do not strike me as having much of a practical turn of mind."

Hans smiled slightly. "I am probably the only one who takes a close interest in his country estate. The others no doubt see me as more of a farmer than a financier!"

"If anyone dares —" bristled Richenda, but Hans laid a restraining hand on her arm.

"Let Euphemia continue. She seems unusually unsure of herself."

"I have to admit, after getting so much wrong in my last escapade, I am wary of jumping to the wrong conclusions."

"There's a first time for everything," said Rory quietly, but not too quietly that I did not hear him.

"The older body was not caught in the previous fire, was it?" I asked. "It was much older?"

"Good grief, Euphemia," said Hans. "I did know that, but the Chief Inspector swore me to secrecy. I was the one who found it."

"That must be her," I said to myself.

"Explain," said Rory coldly.

"My maid, Enid, told me a story about the Wailing Nanny. Apparently the staff thought she was walking abroad again."

"A castle ghost," breathed Richenda.

I shook my head. "There has to be a rational explanation, but I confess I cannot see it yet."

"A warning about the fire!" said Richenda.

"Oh shut up, Richie," said Bertram. "I've been around enough dead bodies now to know there are no ghosts."

"I mean that she told me the story because something odd was happening, but I can't see how the

180

noises are connected. The story," I continued quickly before anyone else broke in, "is that last Laird . . ."

"That obnoxious little man at the wedding?"

"Yes, the one escorting his father, the previous Laird —" I looked at Rory, confused.

"The old man is the Laird, technically," said Rory, "but his son acts as if he is in charge."

"In that case the Laird's son ran away from home when he was very young — a toddler."

"And the nanny went mad with grief?" said Rory scornfully.

"Not exactly. I mean, obviously he came back. Enid said he had climbed into the caravan of a tinker."

"A *what*?" asked Bertram.

"A gypsy," said Rory.

"But he was too little to tell them who he was and too scruffy for them to realise he was the Laird's son."

"Or that's what they said," said Rory darkly. "I can see how he could have sneaked off with them without their knowing, but tinkers aren't necessarily treated kindly here."

"You mean they could have been accused of kidnapping him?" asked Hans.

Rory nodded. "I can imagine they had quite a big discussion about what to do with him before they eventually brought him back."

"But they would not have hurt a child!" cried Richenda, eyes brimming.

"I doubt it, my dear," said Hans quickly, "but they might have decided to raise him as their own." He gave Bertram, who was about to protest, a stern look.

"Absolutely," said Bertram obediently, with a wary eye on the tearful Richenda.

"But when he came back the Wailing Nanny was gone. The Laird put it about he had turned her out, but the staff seemed to believe she had thrown herself from the walls in grief — hence the wailing."

"Aye, I heard that story," said Rory. "All these big old houses have their legends. Stories to frighten wayward maids away from straying at night. Obviously nonsense, as they never found a body."

"Until now," I said. "I think she is the body buried in the wall."

"But who killed her?" asked Bertram.

"I can only guess," I said. "It might have been the Laird, or even his wife, overcome with anger and loss of their son. They would have assumed the boy was dead and it was her fault. And," I hesitated here and looked at Richenda, "the Laird's wife was so upset she lost the child she was carrying."

"So one of them killed her?" asked Rory sceptically.

"It might not have been meant," I said.

Hans interrupted. "It makes sense that it was the body of the missing nanny, or it may once the police have an idea of the age of the bones. It even makes sense that someone might have set the fire in the hope of stopping Stapleford's refurbishment of the building. They might have thought that he would give up on it."

"Or even move away," said Bertram thoughtfully. "We have not known Lucinda for long, but she seems the kind of girl that could be convinced a place was ill-omened or some such rot."

"But the body was discovered because of the fire," said Richenda.

"I know," I said, "but I do not think that was the idea. I think Hans is right, and that the fire was meant to put Richard off rebuilding it or, indeed, from living here."

"So you think whoever murdered the Nanny started the fire?" asked Rory. "Would they not be very old by now?"

"Maybe the fire was set not by the murderer, but by his descendent?" asked Richenda.

A sudden silence fell as we all looked at her. "What?" she said. "I do sometimes get it right!"

CHAPTER
TWENTY-SEVEN

Rory is bait

"It can never be simple, can it?" said Rory.

"I don't suppose the man they found — the one who owned the tie-pin — could have been the one who set the fire?" said Bertram hopefully.

"That would be nice and neat," said Hans.

"And completely unlike real life," said Rory.

"Ellie did have a remarkable reaction to the tie-pin," said Richenda. Then she gave a smug little grin, and flicked back a lock of hair that had become loose. "I am on good form today!"

"That could be no more than the usual sensibilities of a young woman confronted with the remains of any ugly death and possible murder," said Hans.

"What do you mean by that?" asked Richenda, her tone suddenly sharp.

"Most of the weaker sex are somewhat shocked by sudden death," said Bertram uneasily.

"Or simply lacking the experience of the ladies present," said Rory.

"I agree," I said calmly before Richenda could respond, "we are somewhat used to the unusual, but I still find her reaction worthy of study."

"I suppose there must be something we can do?" opined Bertram.

"If there is any way the nursery maid looking after my daughter might be involved," said Richenda hotly, "I want to know."

"It is an avenue worth following," said Hans. "But what can we do?"

"That's easy," said Richenda. "Rory can have a little chat with her."

"Rory?" I asked.

"You must have noticed," said Richenda. "All the female servants want to spend time with Bertram's tall, handsome butler. I imagine he is quite a favourite below stairs." She then pulled a face that was as close as I have ever seen Richenda come to simpering. The reaction of the men in the room was quite startling. Hans looked annoyed, while Bertram and Rory appeared revolted.

"We all have to do our duty for justice to be served," said Richenda piously.

"I could ask Enid if we could visit her grandmother?" I suggested. "She would have been working at the castle when the nanny went missing, and might have some insights to offer."

"I'll tackle that," piped up Richenda. "If you're going to be interviewing an older woman, a married woman like myself should go."

"Really, there is no need to trouble yourself," I protested.

"Actually, it might be better if Richenda spoke to her," said Hans. "Although with Richenda's state borne in mind the woman would need to come to the castle."

"Much nicer than visiting some smelly peasant's cottage," said Richenda, placidly.

"There is no need for Richenda to be troubled at all," I said crossly.

"There is no need to feel left out, Euphemia," said Bertram. "It's just that the old woman might be more comfortable talking about certain things with a more worldly lady."

"He means if there were any shenanigans happening in the castle at the time," said Hans obscurely.

It took me a moment to catch on. "You mean she might know if the nanny was involved with a male member of staff, or even one of the family?" I said.

"Exactly," said Rory, "and your maidenly ears would not be thought fit to hear such things."

At this point, I could have brought up my education in a London brothel,[1] but, as Bertram had also been involved, it seemed a bit unfair. The same thought appeared to have crossed his mind, because he appeared to be trying to shake his head subtly and mouth the words "Please, no" at me. His eyes were rolling like those of a frightened horse.

"What *is* the matter with you, Bertie?" asked Richenda. "Are you having a fit?"

"Itch in my ear," said Bertram, pulling frantically on his left one.

"Besides, I will need your help, Euphemia," said Rory.

"What?" I asked, horrified.

---

[1] All theoretical, I should add.

"I'll need you to be listening in for me. I don't want to be sued for breach of promise. Susie Ellis had the smell of desperation about her before; if she is in any way involved in what has happened, it will have only made it worse."

"That is a most ungentlemanly thing to say," objected Hans.

Rory gave him a level look. "It's your wife that wants me to do this and it's you that hired this girl on a whim."

Hans looked very much taken aback. He was not, after all, used to the free manner Rory tended to speak in when we were investigating some incident. Nor, of course, was he privy to all the escapades we had entered upon together. Bertram shrugged apologetically.

"Right, Euphemia," said Rory. "We had better get on with it."

"What am I to do?" asked Bertram.

"The best thing you and Hans can do is to partake of some after dinner sustenance with the guests and see if you can ferret out any further information about last night," said Rory.

"Particularly where people were," I added.

"And you will need to be discreet," said Richenda without any sense of irony. "I will arrange with Enid for her grandmother to call upon me tomorrow morning."

Rory had already risen to leave. I rose too. "It is possible," I said, "that Stone may ring while I am engaged with some information. If he does, Hans, please understand that he was following my orders and that I bear any blame you may feel needs casting."

"Euphemia," began Hans, but I was already out the door, with Rory on my heels.

"What did you do?" Rory asked me. I explained. He nodded. "Should have been done in the first place," was his only comment.

"So how do we go about this?" I asked.

"It's not that late," said Rory, "so I should be able to convince Susie Ellis to come for a walk with me. She's been hinting about wanting to see the local scenery for some time."

"I remember Merry being rather partial to views," I said. "By which she meant walking out with a footman."

"It appears to be a common euphemism," said Rory blandly.

"Am I supposed to lurk behind a tree?" I asked, with a marked lack of enthusiasm. "It sounds as if there is a sharp wind blowing tonight. It may be difficult to hear your conversation. Though I suppose I am only there for form's sake."

"Would you be willing to swear that I had said what I told you I had said?"

"I would be willing to swear to your character, but not to words I have not heard. That would not be right," I said.

Rory growled with annoyance. "Right, we will have to do something inside. I only hope she does not try to get me into a bedroom."

I laughed. "A big man like you, afraid of a tiny nursery maid?" I said, for it was true that Ellie was of no great height.

"Yer have nae idea what power yous women wield, do yer?"

"You must be frightened," I said. "You are going all Scotch."

Rory made another growling noise and stormed off, so that I had to half walk, half run to keep up with him. When we reached the green baize door, nearest to the library, Rory told me to wait in one of the alcoves. "It's about the only room I can guarantee that Stapleford won't enter."

"Even after dinner?"

Rory snorted. "He has a smoking room and a billiard room for that. I suspect the books make him nervous. Yon Ellie, on the other hand, seems to like the room. I've found her in here on more than one occasion."

"If you're going to sweet-talk her I think you should call her Susie."

Rory snorted and disappeared into the servants' quarters. I found myself a seat and curled up with a book of poetry to wait for developments. To my surprise, he returned only minutes later. "I've left her a note asking her to meet me here." He drew back a set of drapes from one window. Moonlight flooded the room. "She will find it romantic," he said, his mouth curling in a sneer. I went back to my poetry, leaving Rory to pace the room. Despite the fact we had once been close, I found it difficult to read his mood and retiring gracefully into the background seemed the best way forward. I tucked my feet underneath me in a way that would have made my mother faint at my lack of deportment. If Rory stayed at his end of the library, I was fairly certain I could not be seen. Time passed. Rory's pacing increased in speed. I was tempted to tease him, that perhaps his charms were not as great as Richenda thought, but as I was about to open my mouth our eyes met and I decided not to say anything. For whatever reason, Rory was decidedly angry.

"Perhaps we should . . ." I began, when Rory held up his hand, his head on one side. His hearing must be more acute than mine[1] for a moment later, the library door opened and I heard the sound of light, quick steps. I found I could peek around the edge of the window recess.

Ellie crossed quickly to Rory. "I came as soon as I could, Mr McLeod. I had to ensure the child was tucked up safely and I had a maid in attendance of her."

"I am glad to see you take your charge so seriously," said Rory. All traces of anger had vanished and, instead, a slight smile curled his lips. He held out his hands to Ellie. She took two faltering steps towards him. A shy smile echoed his. Very lightly she touched her hands to his. Rory took them in his.

I must have eaten something underdone that evening as I found myself being assailed by indigestion. I could not otherwise account for the sudden and sharp pain that struck in my chest.

"Why, Mr McLeod," said Ellie in a rather sickly voice. "Is this a declaration?"

Bile rose in my mouth.

---

[1] Excellent hearing being a prerequisite for a good butler, for knowing which rooms *not* to enter.

"I am concerned about you," said Rory, looking down at her. "This is a difficult time and your reaction earlier today was extreme."

"Yes, it has been terrible. I am sure we are all upset," said Ellie, in a colder voice. She moved as if to pull away, but Rory held her hands firm.

"I care about you, Susie," he said in a gentle voice. "It upset me greatly to see you so distressed."

Ellie shook her head and tried again to pull away. "I don't want to think about it," she said, sounding as if she was on the edge of tears.

"Oh, Susie, there is something wrong, isn't there? You can tell me. I will look out for you."

Ellie raised her face to his. "If only I could trust you," she breathed.

"But you can," said Rory. "We have known each other such a short time, but sometimes when you meet someone you know, don't you?" He raised one of her hands to his face and brushed her fingers to his lips.

I was, by now, feeling distinctly uncomfortable. I doubted I could say under oath that Rory was not encouraging her, should this come to a breach of promise suit. In fact this was totally not the way I had expected him to take this scene. Rory might be many things, but I had never seen him actively deceive someone like this. I began to feel rather sorry for the nursery maid.

"You have a difficult life, Susie," said Rory. "Your brother . . . he seemed, forgive me, ill-mannered. I fear he exercises too much control in your life."

Susie gave a little sob. "You cannot understand."

"Oh, I think I can. You are not that different from Mrs Muller. Until her marriage, she was very much under the sway of her twin who, as I expect you've discovered, is not a very nice man. But now she has escaped to marriage she has blossomed. It is hard to be a spinster dependent on your employers' whims, and, for a woman like you, who loves children, not having your own establishment and the chance to raise your own must be hard."

Ellie swallowed and nodded.

"I take it your family was very poor? That you have made the best of yourself, but your brother . . ."

"He never wanted to enter service," said Ellie in a quiet voice.

"What did he want?" asked Rory kindly.

"To make his fortune," she said sadly. "He was always sure his luck would turn."

Luck. I thought suddenly of the tie-pin. A horseshoe could be a symbol for luck. But why would he be here? I willed Rory to follow my train of thought, but Rory was far, far ahead of me.

"I assume he asked you to help him?"

Ellie nodded, her head now bowed.

"What did he ask you to do, Susie?"

I noted the use of the past tense. I was on the edge of my seat now.

"To tell him about where I worked," said Ellie, in a voice barely above a whisper.

"To tell him what your employers owned?"

Ellie nodded.

"Susie, are you telling me your brother was a thief?"

"I swear the first time he asked me I didn't understand," said Ellie urgently. "I thought he was proud of me in my new position. I had no idea he would pass on what I told him to help his friends rob the house."

"But when it had happened once he told you that you were a criminal too?"

The girl nodded again.

"But, Susie, you weren't. You say you helped him in innocence?"

"Yes, but he told me the London gang he worked with wouldn't see it like that," said Ellie. "He said they knew I was involved and if I told the police they would make sure I regretted it."

"London gang?" asked Rory. "My dear, much as I want to believe you, I cannot see how a London gang would be working this far north. If you want me to think you innocent of . . ."

"The Mullers were the target," said Ellie. "But when we learned he was putting in the electricity, we knew there would be too many people about for us to . . . to . . ."

"But he followed you up here? You were meeting him? That was why you were in the wrong place so often?"

"Yes," said Ellie, choking on a sob. "When he heard I was going to a castle he thought this was his lucky chance. He thought he could get something expensive without the gang; that I would have access to jewels or something like that." She sighed heavily. "He always was the chancer."

"So what did you do, sweetheart?"

I held my breath. Was using that term of endearment not going too far?

This time Ellie did manage to pull her hands away and step back. "Do?" she asked in a firmer voice.

Rory took a pace forward. It was like watching some kind of odd dance. "It was meant to be a distraction, wasn't it?" he said, still using a gentle voice. "I don't believe you meant to hurt anyone."

"What?" said Ellie in a harsh voice.

"Which one of you set the fire?" asked Rory. "You can tell me, Susie. You can trust me."

"Is that what you think of me? That I would endanger a child or let him endanger a child for the sake of — of riches I don't even believe exist?" Her voice rose higher. "You think we set the fire!"

"Susie, tell me where your brother is and I will help you sort all this out," said Rory. "I can see you have been used, and I . . ."

"He's dead," said Ellie flatly. "It was his body they found in the outbuilding."

I had understood this a few moments ago, but Rory, who I had assumed was thinking along the same lines as me, appeared somewhat thrown.

"Dead," he echoed blankly. "But then . . . who?"

"This was all about trying to get me to confess, wasn't it?" said Ellie. "Trying to make a good impression on Sir Richard, are you? Looking to move up in the world at my expense? Pretending you care for me. Why, you're no better than he was!"

"I am sorry for your loss," said Rory, but he was clearly still reeling from what she had told him. "You must be devastated."

"And stupid. Stupid to think any man would look out for anyone other than himself. You might have got my story out of me, Rory McLeod, but if you breathe a word to anyone I shall deny everything. Why, I shall say you made inappropriate advances to me and, when I refused you, you wanted revenge. You already have quite a reputation below stairs. Shall we see who shall be believed?"

I stepped down from my seat. "Unfortunately, Miss Ellis, every word you said I overheard."

Ellie looked from one of us to the other. Her face contorted in anger. "Don't you see he's using you, too? Men are all alike and he's —"

"I think that is quite enough," I said. I rang the bell. "I think the best thing for you will be to tell the Chief Inspector everything you have told Mr McLeod. If it helps him solve the mystery of the fire, I expect he will take into consideration that you were coerced into helping your brother. We will both speak for you. Considering your recent loss, it may be that he will be kind enough to ensure no charges are pressed. Your best chance now is to cooperate."

All at once, the fight seemed to go out of her and Ellie sank down onto a chair. "What will become of me?" she said in a low voice. "No one will employ me now."

"You should have —" began Rory, but I shushed him. I understood in a way he could not how difficult it

195

was for a woman, without money or a family to support her, to make her way in the world.

When a servant answered the bell I bade him summon the sergeant, who came and took Ellie away. I stopped Rory from following. "It really will go better for her if she owns up," I said. "You surprised me here. You were quite the interrogator."

"By holding her hands," said Rory, "it was easier to tell what she was feeling and when she was lying."

"That is despicable," I said.

Rory shrugged. "It was your friend, Fitzroy, who showed me the trick. You appear to have no problems with him."

"He works for King and Country," I protested.

"And we are trying to act for justice," said Rory. "Is that not an equally noble motive?"

"You are not like Fitzroy," I cried. Unexpectedly, my eyes brimmed with tears.

CHAPTER
TWENTY-EIGHT

Secrets uncovered

I did not expect to get to bed at a reasonable time that night. I waited up for the Chief Inspector's summons. He struck me as a man who did not retire early when involved on a case and I was right. He saw me alone, without his sergeant and without Rory.

"I believe I may owe you an apology, Miss St John," were his opening words.

"Indeed," I said. I had no intention of making it easy for him.

"I have been able to contact various agencies down south and I have been told that not only should I disregard your previous arrest, but that I should treat anything you tell me with the most serious consideration. It seems you are known to people further up the food chain than myself and that they think highly of you." He paused. I got the impression he was looking to me to explain this remarkable communication.

"I am afraid I cannot talk about it," I said with vast satisfaction.

The Chief Inspector struggled not to look impressed. "So do you believe that Susie Ellis set the fire, with or without the aid of her brother?"

"You mean she might have been looking to rid herself of him as a burden?" I asked thoughtfully. "I suppose it would have been a good opportunity to do so. No one knew them up here and it would explain why everything went so wrong. It would hardly have been something she was able to plan. I suppose you have ruled out the possibility that this fire was an accident entirely?"

"Stapleford got some specialist chappie on site who reckons he can pinpoint where the fire took hold. It certainly seems deliberate."

"It would seem a little cold to attempt to burn your brother to death."

"It was the smoke that did it for him," said Stewart. "And in my experience, miss, murderers don't tend to be of the caring type."

I gave him a swift smile. "Women, I believe, prefer to murder at a distance — poison and the like. But in this case, I think Susie Ellis was completely under the sway of her brother. If she had turned on him, I would expect it to be something both sudden and unsuccessful. Besides, she made a strong point of how she would never endanger a child and I believe that. Frankly, I do not think she has the imagination to think of murdering her brother."

The Chief Inspector raised an eyebrow. "I am inclined to agree with you," he said. "I doubt we will ever be able to rule out the possibility of her brother attempting to set the fire to set up a diversion so he could rob the building. I have questioned her closely and she believes she had been able to withstand giving her brother the evidence he needed to move ahead with the robbery."

"But he could have taken a chance anyway."

Stewart nodded.

"He could, but we can hardly ask him."

"And it does not solve the mystery of the previous fire nor of the body in the wall — if there is any link between them."

"I pulled the report from the time and there was nothing to suggest that the previous fire was anything other than an accident. All in all, it was fortunate there were no fatalities. It was suggested that either a fire had been left unquenched, sparking and causing a rug to catch light, or that a discarded cigar had done the job. Whatever it was, the fire started in the servants' quarters.[1]."

"And thus no apparent motive for setting another fire?"

"If it was not Ellis' brother — real name Archibald Timpkins, by the way — then the only obvious motive would be to deter Stapleford from developing that block further. A move that backfired."

"You mean someone who knew about the body in the wall and was attempting to ensure it was not found?"

"Exactly, Miss St John. You are a very insightful young lady. Can I politely suggest that you take care. If we are dealing with the second situation I would ask

_____

[1] In other words, either the housekeeper or the butler would be held to blame.

you to bring anything you uncover straight to me, rather than trying to investigate it yourself. I do not doubt your intellect but, in my experience, people who are seeking to protect old secrets are not only uncommonly devious, they are uncommonly ruthless. This old secret, whatever it is, has been kept for many years, and I am certain whoever is holding it will not hesitate to protect that silence in any way he or she can."

At this point, I considered telling him about the story of the Wailing Nanny. If only I had, perhaps things might have ended entirely differently.

I returned to the small sitting room, which had become our base. I explained, with help from Rory, what had happened with Ellie and about my interview with the Chief Inspector to Richenda, Hans and Bertram. Rory skimmed over what was actually said between him and Ellie, and I did not fill this in. I also did not comment on the Chief Inspector's findings about myself. Bertram and Rory had also signed the Official Secrets Act, and Richenda was aware the three of us got *up to things* at times, but Hans was entirely in the dark about it all.

"I have only to add to this that I spoke to Stone while you were away," said Hans. "On your instructions he sent urgent telegrams to all the references on Mrs Ellis' letter. No one had heard of her."

"But you spoke to one of them," protested Richenda.

"I asked the operator for a number I was given, and assumed the person on the other end was the correct reference. It was undoubtedly an accomplice of her brother. The level of wickedness is quite astounding," said Hans.[1]

"So it's possible the brother set the fire?" asked Bertram in a disappointed voice. "I was hoping there was more to it than that." Hans gave him an odd look.

Richenda patted her half-brother's knee. "Enid is going to ask her grandmother to call on me tomorrow. It may be that there are other stories to unearth. We still have no idea who the body in the wall is."

Bertram visibly brightened. "Oh, good. Still something to work on."

Hans looked slowly around the room. "You are all quite mad," he said.

---

[1] Secretly I wondered what he would think of the levels of wickedness I had previously encountered. To me it seemed forging a reference with a view to gathering information for a robbery was quite mild. I did, sensibly, keep these thoughts to myself.

CHAPTER
TWENTY-NINE

An unhappy parting

The next morning, when Enid drew back the curtains, light flooded through the window in a strange eerie softness. I sat up in bed, yawning, for I had not slept well.

"Has it snowed, Enid?" I asked.

"Just a wee drop."

I got up, wrapping my robe around me and went to the window. Far below me, one of the gardeners or odd job men was pulling burnt wood out of the ashy ruins that had been designed as the new stable block. Every time he took a step the snow rose to the top of his wellingtons. "It must be eight or ten inches," I said.

"Aye, a wee drop," said Enid.

"I take it your grandmother will not be joining us today?"

"She'll take her time," said the maid. "I don't think she'll get Grandpa out to drive the dog cart. He has a bad chest, you see. She'll probably walk up. It's only a mile or so. And it's not like she will be carrying anything."

"Make sure she has a hot cup of tea and a rest before she comes up to Mrs Muller," was all I could think to say. I knew people were hardy in this part of the world, but even I, in my twenties, would not fancy the idea of trudging a mile in snow that deep.

"Depends what you are used to," was Rory's opinion when I managed to catch a word en route to the breakfast.

"How are they taking Ellie's arrest below stairs?" I asked.

"It's all very exciting for them," said Rory. "All very interesting now it's nothing to do with the locals."

"No sense from anyone that there is more to the story?"

Rory shrugged. "I think they are all happy to see what they think is the back of the business."

"But what about the other body?"

"No one is talking about that," said Rory. "It's all that Sassenach maid; knew she were wrong and things like that. Seems others had noticed her wanderings and the way she kept apart from the other staff, to be honest like most nursery maids would, is now seen as a sign of her guilt."

"I think it's very odd none of them are talking about the body in the wall. Very suspicious. How's Mrs Lewis?"

"In a bit of a daze. Cook had to ask her twice for today's menus."

"They're not giving you a hard time, are they?"

Rory grinned, his translucent green eyes lighting up, "Why should they? I'm one of their own, after all." As he said this in a ridiculously refined accent rather than his own Scottish lilt I had to laugh. "You'd better go into breakfast before people see you dallying with the handsome valet," he said.

I gave him a grin and crossed the threshold in good humour. The spread set out on the buffets was vast and the table to seat us all equally so. As usual, the married women had stayed to have breakfast in bed. A small cluster of financiers huddled together attacking their sausages and bemoaning whether they would be able to get out of this "snow-bound hell hole". At the far end of the table sat Bertram, staring mournfully at two carefully filleted kippers. I gathered a plate of scrambled eggs, two kidneys and three rashers of bacon, intending to sit down beside him.

A hand on my shoulder stopped me and a voice spoke close to my ear. "I hear you have wound the Inspector around your little finger as usual, Euphemia," said Richard Stapleford. "He may be convinced of your innocence, but I am sure there will be others who will begin to notice that wherever you go, trouble follows."

"How lovely to see you, Sir Richard," I said loudly. "I trust your wife is well?"

Richard kept his voice low. "Oh, she is proving most satisfactory. Surprisingly, she has confessed to me she had qualms about our marriage and that you persuaded her to go forward with it." He smiled broadly at me, but his low voice was tinged with menace. "Do not think for a moment that this would make me look favourably on your marriage to my step-brother."

"Bertram?" I said, astonished.

"I know full well you have Muller in the palm of your hand — and in your bed, too. But Richenda is giving him an heir and even your charms cannot compete with that. Be aware that if you turn your greedy eyes towards Bertram, I will ensure, with the utmost finality, that your wedding will never come to pass."

"You are despicable," I said softly. Then more loudly, I said, "I will not keep you from her a moment longer." And I strode over to Bertram and sat down. I could feel myself trembling from head to toe.

"Hello, Euphemia," he said dully. "You look like you have a fine appetite."

"It's the cold," I said, struggling to appear normal. I could feel Richard's gaze on the back of my head. "It might be roaringly warm in front of the fires, but more than two feet away and it's freezing. As for the passages, it is as if they play host to very windy ghosts."

"People who died of indigestion?" asked Bertram.

"Such a boyish sense of humour." Hans sat down beside him. "Despite the snow, Mrs Andrews, Enid's grandmother, has arrived. I inferred from her hostile looks that it is not the place of a husband to take breakfast with his wife, nor to listen in to the gossip among the womenfolk."

"By 'gossip' you mean 'vital exchange of information'," I said with a smile.

"Yes, I wouldn't tell Richenda you think she gossips," said Bertram. "She'd be very cross."

"Nonsense," said Hans, "She would be delighted I was implying she has plenty of friends to gossip among."

"She does seem rather lonely," I said. "I am trying to interest her in hosting dinners."

"An excellent idea," said Hans. "Once she has had the baby she will have much to discuss with the local matrons. Adorable though Amy is, she is not a child one might choose to discuss . . ."

"All tantrums and tears?" asked Bertram.

"Toddlers are usually left to nursery maids until they develop manners," I said. "Whereas babies are cooed over by everyone."

"Just as well you know about these things, Euphemia," said Bertram. "Or you might feel a bit left out once the new 'un arrives. I mean, will Richenda even need a companion then? And if she's to become a hostess . . ."

"Euphemia will always have a home with us," said Hans shortly.

"Doesn't your mother want you to come to live with her when she marries her bishop?" asked Bertram. I clenched my hands under the table — I could have kicked him.

"Your mother is marrying a bishop?" repeated Hans, surprised. "If indeed she is in a position to house you, and you wanted to go, as much as I would wish you to remain at the Muller estate, I could not in good conscience keep you from your family if you wished to return. When is the marriage?"

I shot dagger looks at Bertram, who belatedly got the message and, shrinking in his seat, mouthed apologies at me.

"It is all a long time in the future," I lied, for I knew my mother was marrying in a few weeks. "I am sure

Richenda will be glad of my company whilst she is . . . increasing."

Hans smiled warmly at me. "Indeed, I am certain you will be of the utmost comfort to her."

We all ate in silence, listening to the discontented murmurings of the bankers. After eating his usual two boiled eggs and two slices of toast, Hans rose and bade us farewell. "I confess I am curious to know what the old lady has told Richenda. You and Bertram have quite infected me with your curiosity," he said. "Shall we meet before luncheon in that little parlour and discuss what we have discovered? Richenda tends to need a short rest after breakfast now she is pregnant."

"Always did," said Bertram under his breath.

"An excellent idea, Hans," I said, smiling at him. He gave me a short bow and left the room. Immediately I turned on Bertram. "Thank you for that," I hissed between gritted teeth. "You have no idea how long and how hard I have worked to forge my own way in the world. I do not appreciate the suggestion that I might be parcelled up and returned to my mother so she can marry me off to one of her friends' idiot sons."

Bertram, who had been mid crumpet, spluttered crumbs all over the table. "Euphemia! I'm sorry. I never thought!"

Richard had already put my nerves on edge and Bertram's unthinking comments were the last straw. I fairly spat at him. "I told you something in confidence and you blurt it out to Hans. I thought you were my friend." I knew as I said this I was being unfair. I recalled all too well how I had thrown my mother's marriage at Bertram's head in a fit of pique, but I was frightened. "You are a man. You have your independence. You have no idea what it is like to be beholden to others."

"So you don't mind being beholden to my sister's husband?" snapped Bertram. "It has looked to me on more than one occasion that you and Hans are rather close. Even Rory has remarked on it."

"Well, if *Rory* has remarked on it," I said, my temper rising ever higher. "Rory, that paragon of virtue, who jilted me for no good reason, but still it seems harbours an unwonted possessiveness over my person, then it must be true. That you have known me for years and know me to be of good character means nothing."

"Of good character," said Bertram, his face reddening. "You pulled a policeman off his horse!"

"I had good reason!"

"I had to rescue you from a brothel!"

"You did not have to rescue me, I was . . ." I stopped, suddenly aware that the background noise had ceased. I turned to see all the financiers and some of the other guests who had ventured downstairs staring at us. Tears pricked the back of my eyes. I threw Bertram one last look of pure hatred and ran from the room.

CHAPTER
THIRTY

A shooting

Unshed tears blinded me. I stumbled into a gentleman, who caught me by the elbows. "Excuse me," I said, trying to pull away. "I need to . . ."

"Goodness, you seem rather distressed, my dear," said a vaguely familiar voice.

I blinked back the tears and realised I had run straight into the Laird's son, Dougal Kennedy. "I am so sorry," I began.

"Think nothing of it," said Dougal. "In fact this is quite serendipitous. I have been wanting a word with you."

"With me?" I said, astonished.

"It is quite a delicate matter. Perhaps we could step out of the corridor?"

I hesitated.

"Good heavens, you cannot surely fear for your reputation? I am the Laird's son!"

"Well no," I began, but certain ideas were beginning to form in my mind. This was the little boy who had run away with the gypsies.

"Let us go in here," he said opening a door, seemingly at random. He ushered me into a small antechamber that seemed to serve little purpose. It also had only the one exit.

"Perhaps you could leave the door open," I said. "It would make me feel more comfortable."

He frowned, but then quickly smiled. "I will leave it ajar. After all, what is the point of a private conversation if all and sundry can hear it? But if it will make you feel more comfortable . . ." He left the door open the merest crack.

"It would be most seemly if my employer, Mrs Muller, were also with me. I am unmarried."

"And yet, you chat happily with men at breakfast."

"Gentlemen, who I know well," I countered. He was between the door and I. How had that happened?

"But it is Mrs Muller I need to speak to you about. I understand she has sent for Mrs Andrews, the grandmother of one of the maids here and a retired member of my father's staff."

"Yes," I said. The hairs on the back of my neck rose as the pieces began to fall into place.

"I feel I need to advise you that Mrs Andrews did not leave my father's employ on good terms and thus anything she has to say should be treated with scepticism."

"Anything?" I countered. "Or merely when she discusses your family?"

"Truth be told, the old woman should be in an asylum. She has the strangest fantasies. I told my father he should have had her locked up years ago, but he wouldn't hear of it."

"Perhaps he was worried she might have told her tales to her daughter, or even her granddaughter."

"Oh, Agnes is a good girl. Very fond of the family. I doubt she would want to make trouble, but Enid . . . I regret to say it, but she takes after her grandmother. A flighty one."

"You ran away with the gypsies when you were little, didn't you?" I asked. "Why did you do that?"

"Oh, that old story." Dougal Kennedy shrugged his shoulders casually, but his eyes never left my face. "I don't recall. I am sure it seemed like a grand adventure at the time."

"Your nanny was very upset, I believe."

"Yes, poor old Mason. I believe she was quite distraught. Left in a flood of tears, my father said. Of course, he wrote to her afterwards and told her I had been found."

"Did he? Where did she go?" I asked.

"Home. Inverness, I think."

"Does your father still have her address?"

"My dear girl, we are not in the habit of keeping in touch with former servants who are not on our pension," said Dougal with a cold smile.

"So what is it you wish me to do?" I asked.

"I think it would be better if Mrs Muller was not disturbed by Mrs Andrews' tales. Perhaps you could suggest to her that the meeting need not take place? The last thing a lady in her position needs is to be confused and frightened by silly Highland ghost stories."

"I believe they are together at this very moment."

Dougal Kennedy's mask slipped for a moment. "Damn it," he cried. He took three paces towards me until we were only inches apart. I was backed against the panelling. I used all my will power not to flinch from him. "I really, really need you to help me out here, miss," he said. "My family has lost this castle, but we still have a name in the area, a reputation to uphold. Stapleford may have bought this house, but my father is still the Laird."

"I do not think Sir Richard understands the matter quite like that."

"I don't care what that dolt thinks!" shouted Dougal, backing into the room and clenching his fists. "My family has held this land for generations and our word is law!"

"I rather think the Chief Inspector would disagree." I tried to edge sideways towards the door. "Was it an accident?" I asked. "I imagine your father thought you were dead. He must have been beside himself with grief."

"Hah!" said Dougal. "My father needed his heir. My mother was too frail to bear another son. He was angry. Rightfully so. Mason had failed in her duties. All she had to do was keep me safe, but let me out of her sight and the gypsies took me. If I had not run away from them, who knows what might have happened to me? We have never welcomed those people on our lands."

"So you are saying they kidnapped you? It was not that you ran away? Ran away because your father had a temper?" I ventured a guess.

The change that came over Dougal froze me to the spot. "Father only ever did what was best for me. The Laird must behave correctly. Boys don't always understand that. Sometimes it has to be beaten into them."

"Did he beat your mother?" I asked. "Is that why there were no more children?"

"Mother was from the lowlands. She found the climate up here too harsh."

"I see," I said with obvious doubt. "Did he beat his servants?"

"Only when they deserved it. It is the way up here. It is understood."

"But he went too far with Mason, did he not? He killed her?"

"Stupid English maid. A Scottish girl would have taken the beating and been glad she had not been turned out. That was all he was doing. Punishing her. He needed her to look after my mother. He did not mean to kill her."

"So he buried her in the wall. When did he tell you?"

"When he sold the castle."

"He told you it was your fault, did he not?" I said. "If you had not run from your lessons he would not have had to beat her."

The lines of anger on Dougal's face faded. "Oh, you do understand. It was my fault. I had to keep his secret. Keep his reputation intact."

"You did not know there was a man hiding there, did you?"

"No, of course not," said Dougal. "But the Chief Inspector has told me he was a robber, so no great loss."

"His life does not matter? It must have been a horrible way to die," I said.

"It is a shame, but I only did the hangman's job for him," said Dougal. "He should not have been there."

"And the fire you set should only have been bad enough to stop Sir Richard developing the building?"

Dougal turned away from me. "Oh, I don't know," he said. "I don't know what I was thinking! I had to stop them discovering the body until I had a chance to move it, but then I thought, why did Stapleford have the right to sit in our castle while we had to live in a rat-infested old manor in the village?"

"Because you had no more money and he bought the castle from you."

"But it is my birthright," said Dougal firmly. "He has no right to it. It is mine! Mine or no one's."

I think it was then that I realised he was not simply confused but well on the road to madness. "Of course," I said. "I understand you have done nothing wrong. You did not mean to harm Susie Ellis' brother and your father did not mean to kill Nanny Mason." I spoke as if to a young child. "Everything will be all right."

"No! No! It won't be!" cried Dougal. "You will tell them, won't you? You will tell them all everything. I will never get the castle back!" And so saying, he drew a revolver from his pocket. "This is my father's old service revolver," he said calmly. "If he had wanted to kill Mason he would have used this. You do see that, don't you?"

"Of course," I said. The door stood a mere two feet from me. "But you won't make anything better by killing me," I said firmly, although inside it felt as if every nerve and sinew was shaking with fear. "You are an intelligent man. It will only make . . ."

"Shut up!" yelled Dougal. "Shut up! I have to shut you up!"

Then everything happened very quickly. I screamed and dived towards the door. I caught my foot on the rug and sprawled across the floor. A bullet rang out above me, hitting the wall. Then the door burst open. "Euphemia!" cried Bertram, seeing me lying there.

"Bertram, look out. He's got . . ."

But I never got any further. The gun went off again and Bertram slumped to the ground. Rory, a footman and several of the guests who had been at breakfast piled through the door. They wrestled the gun from Dougal. It went off once more, but no one cried out. I did not see if the bullet struck, for I was on my knees by Bertram. His face was waxy. A large pool of red seeped slowly across the rug.

"Bertram!" I cried, but he did not answer me.

To be continued . . .